THE TWELVE MAN BILBO CHOIR

A NOVEL INSPIRED BY ACTUAL EVENTS THAT
CHANGED LEGAL HISTORY.

PETER STAADECKER

ISBN 978-0-9959251-1-3
Paperback Edition 2.0,
March, 2017.

PRAISE FOR THE TWELVE MAN BILBO CHOIR

"... Staadecker is a modern day John Steinbeck ..."

"... utterly compelling and moving ..."

"... I was blown away. Brilliant ..."

"... the characters climbed into my head and invaded my every waking moment ..."

"... what a wild ride ... at times darkly humorous, at times bleakly tragic ..."

"... a book on many, many, many levels; behind the most evident level of mystery, prison escapes and love story I think Staadecker is very subtly debating two contrasting, ancient philosophies ......"

Table of Contents

1. The Backstory

I verified all the facts I could in this story. They all checked out, exactly as told to me. As best I can tell then, the story is gospel. I've set it down here as I first heard it, with only two caveats:

I've had to change names, places, and timelines for to avoid legal problems. And I've watered down some strong language, while still trying to capture the original tone.

The backstory – the story behind the story - starts in the US Deep South. I won't reveal the exact location. That's part of avoiding the legal wrangles.

I was driving northwards and east after a boring conference. I was following backroads with my camera hanging on the empty passenger seat. Against my every rule I picked up a hitchhiker.

It was hot with barely any traffic on the road. I hadn't seen another car for at least twenty minutes. A tough location to wait for a ride. The hitchhiker was on a long straight stretch, so I saw him long before I pulled over.

There was something about his worn clothes, the lines in his face, the subdued patience with which he stood by the dusty road that made me want to stop.

He had one hand out to thumb a ride. His other hand hung at his side, wrapped around the top of what looked like a brown paper sandwich bag and some bottled water. He had a book tucked under that arm and he was wearing a suit that looked far too formal for hitchhiking.

The suit looked like it had seen little wear, but the style was old. The lapel widths, the trouser width, the turn-ups, the double breasted cut all looked like something that had gone out of fashion a decade ago. It was also far too hot a get-up for such a day.

I was overdue to deliver some kindness to someone. I had argued with a number of people over different issues over the last few days, even been provoked into rudeness, and was not well pleased with my recent self-image of cantankerousness.

I was starting to question my own character and whether it was all I wanted it to be. If I argue with two people in the same week, it might be them, it might be justified, it might be a bad week. It might just be random chance. You're always going to run into people who mess up your hotel bookings, are unapologetic, get your restaurant meal orders wrong, don't care, make a hash of plugging that flat car tire, are incompetent, get your registration details wrong on the conference you're attending, or whatever.

But if I argue with four people in four days, I start to ask myself if I'm the common factor. Perhaps we all have moments of doubt and self-reflection like that at some point. I do every few years, and this was one of those moments for me.

So I stopped for him. The first time in twenty years that I've even considered taking a hitchhiker.

He was polite, but for the first many miles, he was reserved and ventured little except that he was traveling north to Maine, where a grown daughter lived. After a visit with the daughter he would cross to the West Coast and stay with his other grown child, a son, in San Francisco. He hadn't seen either for years and all three greatly looked forward to getting together. His wife had died years ago and he was not remarried.

He was somewhere between forty and sixty with a sun-beaten face that made his age hard to judge. He was balding, with closely cropped hair on the side, and clean shaven. His hands were workman's hands, calloused and sunburned. He bore himself with quiet and dignity. He called me "Sir", long after I suggested he use my first name.

He offered to share his sandwich with me. I accepted, to my own surprise, and then bought a lunch and coffee for both of us at the mid-day gas stop in return. He relaxed a little.

I learned over lunch that he was a strict vegetarian, something that surprised me. It was the first inkling I had that he was more complex than I had judged.

I'd guessed him to be an uncomplicated sort by his plain vocabulary, his outdated clothes and lack of car. While we drove, I noticed that he was repeatedly surprised by everyday things we passed: a school playground teeming with little kids, a lush green garden standing out from its brown, dusty surrounding field, a group of young women dressed in bright clothes, a roadside bar advertising cold beer with a flashing neon sign, large 18 wheeler trucks going up the road in the opposite direction, heavy traffic and complex highway interchanges near city limits, even a simple white picket fence with a gate hanging open. All these things he stared at, turning his head to follow them as we passed. It was like riding with a four-year old.

As I came to learn later though, he knew far more of the world than I ever will.

At the end of lunch he carefully bought another set of packaged sandwiches to replace those we'd eaten in the car. He asked if he could get me some for the road too. I said no, faintly surprised at the meticulous care he gave to restocking his sandwiches. I learned much, much later why he needed to do so.

To make up for my curmudgeonly arguments over the past week, I made an effort to tell him something about myself, to be a little more extrovert than my usual self.

I told him about the conference I'd attended, about my decision to make a driving trip to and from the conference, to take some time off afterwards and to take photos on the backroads along the way home.

That evening, still in the Deep South, we were in a mid-sized town. He told me that he planned to sleep on a bench in a Greyhound bus station. He planned to continue hitch hiking in the morning. I told him I'd swing by in the morning and, if he was still in the bus station, I'd give him a ride further. I asked him if I could contribute some dollars to his evening meal, which he declined with embarrassment.

I headed to a motel for the night.

I had a hard time falling asleep, alternatively wondering whether I should have offered to pay a motel room for him, and then telling myself that he wasn't my responsibility. Just when I'd nod off, I'd start recycling through the same thoughts again. I'd say to myself he's an adult, and then I'd remember his childlike wonder at the things we'd passed on the road.

The next day I started early and found him still at the bus station. He accepted the ride and in exchange offered me the story that follows.

Over the next few days of leisurely driving our exchange continued. I bought him meals, and ultimately convinced him to let me pay a motel room for him each night. He continued his story each morning.

This is his story. I have never regretted the exchange we made.

2. Bilbo Correctional Facility

I bin here seven years. The Bilbo Correctional Facility. Named after some previous Chairman of the Board of Corrections down South here, his hifalutin reverency, the honourable, or maybe not, George Z.W. Bilbo.

Not surprising, us inmates think of it as the Dildo Erection Facility, an' the scratching on the wall in the 3-holer outhouse behind the gravel pit says

"Dildo Erection Facility: Get Yours Here".

Good old Z.W. Never met the man, don't know ifn' he's pleased to have a prison named after him an' have his name misspelt in a fly-ridden long-drop. Prob'ly is. At least, to have the prison named after him.

There's a photo of Z.W. hanging at the entrance to the canteen where the cons eat. He looks pretty pleased with life. Nice clothes, fancy ring on his finger, real gold, big gut from too many state-paid meals. I used to wonder ifn' he ever brung his family to see his photo hanging up there like king of the prison.

Because of his big gut, one time some con scrawled underneath the photo "The face that lunched a thousand chips".

Don't know where the con got the pen from. Anyways, the guards cleaned up the writing pretty quick. Ifn' you know where to look, you can still see the traces of the writing there. Still can read it if you look close.

Me, I'd druther have a bar, a chicken fry or even a cat-house name after me, anything but a prison.

Takes all types in this world.

3. Hieronymus

Hieronymus came in on a Friday. That's unusual right there. Norm'ly prisoners are processed by the transfer facility on a Monday. They're assigned a receiving prison. Paperwork gets signed on a Tuesday by both the transfer facility an' the receiving facility. Then the papers (an' the man) get transferred to the receiving facility on the Wednesday, not a Friday.

Prisons run on paperwork. Papers is always more important 'n the man. The papers get filed processed, transferred, accepted, signed, filed, copied, counter-signed, witnessed by bosses, an' again by their bosses, initialed by the chief medic's office (south end of a north-bound horse that he is), by the sheriff, by the state psychologist (there's another useless waste of space), by the head chaplain, by the Corrections Labour an' Education department, by the Transportation Division, by the Stores Division, checked by a whole mess of clerks an' signed again.

The man follows where-ever the paper file takes him. He's already fading into insignificance, compared to the papers.

Tell you another thing. The papers see more free daylight then the man does. The papers fly back an' forth from prosecutor's office to court clerk's office to transfer centres to jails. They sit on desks where the windows have no bars. Where sun shines in. Meanwhile the man is behind some locked door with that purple colour light from a neon tube. Even the neon tube is behind a fine mesh cage so as we don't break it. Prison guards don't want cons loading up with bits of sharp pointy glass.

Paper rules. The man is nothing. Ifn' the paper says the man's gotto move, the man moves. Ifn' the paper says the man's gotto stay, the man stays.

So Friday was unusual. So was Hieronymus. Small guy. Looked harmless. Looked helpless. Thick glasses. Thin an' pale as a statue cased in a century of pigeon crap. Coughing like a terminal pneumonia case. Turned out that was three quarters what it was.

You could see he'd been through some bad stuff, see he didn't belong, no longer cared.

No curiosity.

Now that there's real unusual for a new con. Bilbo is mighty strange to most new cons. Brown and grey. Nothing green except a small patch of grass and roses outside The Warden's window. Carefully looked after by some ancient cons that spend all day bent over that little patch. The rest is grey gravel, from Dildo Correctional's own gravel pit. Spread over brown earth. Grey concrete, grey steel doors, grey barbed-wire fences, grey towers. The sounds are kinda' grey too. Guards shouting one-word commands as they march a work detail to a prison bus, chains clanking on the chain gang. Mutters from a few cons. Someone shouting inside a concrete building where you can't see. 'Cause of the concrete everything echoes. An' neither the cons nor the guards are likely to win beauty pageants. Some of us are down-right ugly looking specimens.

So no curiosity is odd. Unless you're halfways dead. Don't know if Hieronymus was halfways dead or not. I can tell you he was totally drawn into himself. Didn't care much what people said or did. Musta' bin pretty sick at least to care so little about what was going around him. Followed guards' orders an' kept his eyes down an' mouth shut.

4. Homoousios vs. Arianism

I know it was Friday when he came because I write a diary. Dunno why. It'll never see any more light of day than I will. Figger though, ifn' I die in here, there'll be some record somewhere of me. Might never get read by anyone, might never be found, but still.

The writing thing is hard. First off you're not allowed to keep pens or pencils. Guards say letting cons keep sharp things is a risk. Some of them maybe right at that.

Like Zabriski who likes to spit in our soup. He'll get a sharp point someday, might not just be an HB pencil either. Ifn' you're dumb enough to tease the dog, dog will have its day. Just a matter of time. So, I have to wait till Sat'day to write my diary. Sat'day you get 1 hour library pass for compliant behaviour. An' ifn' you're enrolled for study like me you get another 2 hours on Sunday. An' you get the use of a pen that's chained to the library desk where they let you sit.

In case you've never seen a prison library, desks an' bar stools are bolted to the floor. They use bar stools rather than chairs so that you don't pull off a backrest or armrest for a weapon. Also helps that the cons don't ever get comfortable like a real person.

Sometimes the library is empty. Sometimes it's crowded. That's usually before Valentine's Day, Mother's Day, or Christmas, when lots of cons want to write home.

There's a joke in Dildo Correctional about a crowded day in the library. One con gets up from his stool. Doesn't want to lose his spot. Says to the con next to him – I'm going for a crap – will you watch my stool?

Didn't get it at first, not being the swiftest. Cracked

me up when I finally got it.

I'm doing divinity studies. Don't care for it any more than for say, welding or body shop or the public health certificate in food handling for short-order cooks. But. You get a pen ifn' you study. I write my diary when they're not looking.

The thing about divinity studies, it's stuff that people have been wrangling about for thousands of years. Since cave man said "ugg" an' pointed at the sky.

Prb'ly his wife said "whatever, an' put out the trash while you're at it". Women are practical that way. Speak better too. Ar-ti-cu-late it's called.

Funny thing. Some trucks are called ar-ti-cu-late too. Never understood how the same words can mean completely different things like that. Did like the joke 'bout the stool though.

So no one thinks I'm gonna finish studies any time soon, what with me being dumber than Luther an' Zwingli an' Calvin an' Storch an' all those great lightbulbs. So I get to keep coming to the library weekend after weekend. Nobody thinks it's strange no more. I can keep going for the next fifty years. An' I write my diary.

Some days the Chaplain asks how I'm doing. I tell him I'm torn between the posit'n of the Anabaptists an' the Lollards an' what does he think. He scratches his head an' says in that superior bible college accent "Interesting, interesting. That whole pedo-baptim debate has of course led ... eventually ... to much of the divergence between ... umm ... the Evangelicals, the Baptists, Lutherans, Methodists and... hmmm... I'll see if I have any critiques and summaries of those positions. Let me ... hmm ...get back to you. Yes, yes, very interesting area you're looking at."

An' ifn' he ever does start in on that again, I'll tell

him I'm moved on to the Council of Nicaea an' the big fuss over homoousios vs. Arianism, or the Council of Trent, or the Gnostic Gospels, or the Sethian texts, or what does he think of the Nag Hamadi library... "Oh, an' Chaplain, while you're at it – would you mind bringing me some more blank note paper? Thank you kindly, sir."

The other book in the library that I use a lot is "The Child's Book of Victorian Parlour Games", 1878-1888, Volume 3, By Edgar G. Greenlock, reprinted 1907 by Jonathan Harper an' Sons. It's the top shelf at the back of the prison library. Hard to reach. No-one else uses it.

5. Jeb

Dildo Correctional is medium to low security. No real hard cases, not much in the way of serious gangs inside. But prison paperwork makes mistakes sometimes, or judges get confused. Whatever.

Take Jeb. An' I wish you would.

No idea how he got assigned to low to medium security or why he's not on death row. 'Ppears he has a long history of beating on people, ending up with badly injuring a guy who – Jeb says - cheated him at poker. Seems Jeb shouted, "I'll show you poker". Reached behind him for the fireplace poker an' beat the poor fellow.

Jeb's still like that, broody, short fuse. Body like an overgrown bull calf. Disposition like a rattlesnake that's had it tail trod on. I walk wide around him.

On farm labour detail even the guards are uneasy when someone puts a pickaxe or a big shovel in Jeb's hand. They'd rather he had a little hand trowel, like a kid's plastic mini-spade an' bucket at the beach. 'Cept no-one uses those at the farm. No beach here. No life guards, no ice cream lollipops. No worried Mom shouting – not so deep in the water, Buddy!

The guards stand back, an' snick the rifle safety catches to the "off" position soon as he picks up the shovel or pick-axe. Sunglasses or no, you know who they're watching.

That's another reason I walk wide around Jeb. When the brown stuff hits the fan, an' it will, I don't wanna be in the line of fire.

6. Time

I told you I bin here seven years. Easy to say. You can say it in a heartbeat. But to live it takes one tenth of your life away. Ten percent. More ifn' you're unlucky.

'Magine you're seeing a doctor.

He listens to your heart an' says – this is not good – your heart has lost 10 percent of its function since I last saw you.

I dreamt that one time in my cell when I was in solitary.

Prison dreams are strange anyhow, but when you're in solitary the dreams get even stranger.

Said in my dream– doctor how can that be – you just listened to it yest'day?

He just shook his head an' repeated – your heart has lost 10% of its function. It's shrinking a little every day in here. Gonna kill you.

Seven years takes 270 million heartbeats. I worked out. An' ifn' I had a cent for each of those heartbeats, I'd have $2.7 million dollars.

That's the kind of 'rithmetic you got time for doin' ifn' you're doin' time.

In seven years your dorm don't change, your food don't change an' your routine don't change. An' each year after the rainy season, Hoover's farm is just as swampy as it was when your first saw it. You think nothing changes, 'cept maybe your shrinking heart.

But ifn' you get a glimpse of the world outside, that'll remind you how much a real person – not a con - will go through in the outside world in seven years.

Take Valerie. From my dorm window, I get a small view of the parking lot where the prison staff park an' where the bus drops off prison staff in the morning. Ifn' I stand on my toes an' angle my view I can see Valerie arrive in the mornings.

Valerie's the PA to the Warden. Personal Assistant. Real pretty too. I've never got to talk to her in seven years, but she's a looker.

Anyways, when I first came to Dildo, year one, she used to come to work each day by bus. Six months later there was this guy that drops her off by car Monday mornings. Didn't really cotton to him at first, drove a muscle car, slicked back hair, leathers an' such. Still, seemed to make her happy. Lots of hugs an' kisses. Then beginning of year two, I noticed he was dropping her off every day of the week. Figgered after all those weekends together, they'd moved in or even gotten married.

They give each other a kiss an' a smile an' she gets out of the car. Then they wave to each other an' he drives off. Sometimes he drives off first while she stands, watching, smiling, waving. Sometimes he waits in the car smiling, waving, while she walks to the entrance.

I like to watch 'em because she looks happy. They both look happy. It's like I've got an adopted daughter. I'm real happy for her.

Sure enough, by end of year two she's pregnant. In year three, I guess the baby is born because she takes off work for a few months. When she comes back to work I worry for her. Her husband is still driving his two door muscle car. I want to talk to the man, say – what you thinkin' – that's no car to fit a wife an' child in.

The changes are real slow. But somewhere round year four, I notice, it's all change. He pulls up. She gets out. He roars off. Tyres screeching. Kicking up gravel an' smoke.

No kiss, no wave no smiles, nobody waits for nobody. She no longer looks happy.

Wasn't sure I wanted to watch no more. Felt sick about it. Thought about my own daughter an' how it would be ifn' that was happening to her.

'Bout two month later Valerie's arriving by bus all mornings. Never seen the dick-head husband again.

So that's life in the real world: in just four years you date, then you start married life with someone, spend weekends hunting for a house, move in, spend evenings choosing furniture an' painting walls, then you get settled an' you start talking family, looking at the budget, wondering whether a promotion might help or a change of job, maybe night school, making plans together every night, the baby arrives, lots of excitement an' more happiness, redecorations, learning about kids, vaccinations, colic, baby's first smile, first word, first steps, then something goes sour, who knows what, arguments, tears, shouting, doors slamming, hearts breaking, each one curled up on the bed at night, backs to each other, as far away from each other as possible, almost fallin' off the edges of the bed, the marriage breaks up, sell the house an' furniture an' all. An' now there's a tiny kid in the world without a father. An' a new mother tryin' to figger out how to hold it all together. That's just four years in the real world, never mind seven.

But my dorm doesn't change, my routine doesn't change, every Friday night in the canteen is beans an' rice. Like I'm stuck in a bad movie that rewinds every seven days. I've just payed up a tenth of my life with a shrinking heart.

7. Cory

Cory's a genius, a real professor.

Money forgers get caught because of the paper. No matter how good their printing is, their paper's crap. Cory though, he got the real stuff. Now you can't get the real stuff here unless you're government or Fort Knox. It's too tightly controlled.

But Cory used what confidence men call "the little lever". When banknote blanks - that's the paper on which you print - are too hard to forge, you forge something easy that gets you access to the blanks. That's the lever.

I've known Cory ever since I bin here. Wouldn't trust him with anything that's worth anything, but he's OK once he knows you know. Actually like the guy. We like each other. Talk about all kinda' stuff. He says I'm too serious. Says one day he'll teach me how to live for the day.

I saved him from a beating one time by another con. So he talks to me. I've heard the story a few times. Not many have. But it's a good one.

Cory's girlfriend is Brazilian. Seems, over the years the Brazil Feds have moved offices back an' forth between Rio an' Brasilia. Two years ago, they moved out of part of a warehouse in Rio, stayed in the other half. They called it downsizing although they tripled the warehouse space in Brasilia. That's governments for you.

An' guess who rented the empty half back in Rio? So now Cory an' Gracia share a warehouse address with the Brazilian Government Department for Agricultural Improvement. The Feds are in 18 Rua Frederica Bittenkurtz, Unit A, an' Cory's in Unit B. That's part 1 of the lever. But the lever isn't ready yet. Now they forge an RFP, that's request for proposal in business speak, from the Minister of Finance, the Ministério da Fazenda. See, forging a letterhead an' a signature from a minister is a lot easier than making dime-store scratchpads look like banknote blanks.

The RFP is two parts. The first part is a non-disclosure agreement, with an invitation to two Swiss, two German, an' three British companies to bid on supplying a new, more secure banknote blank to the Ministério da Fazenda an' the Brazilian mint, the Casa Da Moeda Do Brasil. A blank means the bidders supply the paper with key security features, but additional printing onto the blank happens elsewhere.

Big words, but I got a good mem'ry. Sometimes it's near what folks call photo-graphic. I've got things floating around in my head that are no use to me from thirty years ago. I can recite them like it was yesterday. I can tell you the name of every kid I went through school grades one to seven with. First name, last name, middle name, which desk they sat in, the class room layout, an' the teachers' names.

Anyhow, I'm telling it like Cory tells it. Using his words. The seven companies are all suppliers of banknotes and blanks to governments throughout the world. They're mighty proud of what they do, an' they're audited by the big standards authority in The Hague to see that their security, an' printing, an' staff an' transport arrangements are good enough.

Condition of seeing the specifications for the new banknote blanks an' participating in the bid part 2, is to first sign the non-disclosure an' return it to Cory at Bittenkurtz 18, Unit B. With proof of their current secure printer certification.

All seven companies sign. Non-disclosures are standard in their business. They want to bid on the business. Non-disclosure means they can't discuss their bids, or even the existence of the RFP, or the outcome with anyone outside of their company. Cory's a genius. He's creating a confidence scam where the victims have just signed a legal agreement not to talk about it. To anyone. Ever.

Now Cory shows them last part of the lever. RFP part 2. The specifications for the new banknote blanks include specs for the paper dimensions, weight, cotton composition, density, a security thread, a hologram thread with "100" repeated all up an' down the thread (for 100 Brazilian reals, says Cory in the RFP).

An' there's got to be a watermark of that Brazilian liberation hero, Joaquim José da Silva Xavier. Ol' Jo Jo, the hero, picture supplied by Cory in the RFP, looks a lot like Benjamin Franklin. The seven companies either don't know or don't care. Cory chose these seven because they have never supplied the US. They also don't realize that the rest of the specs are modelled on the US $100 bill. No other printing on the paper because these are blanks. The Brazilian Mint, Cory tells them, will do the overprinting in Brazil, on top of the blanks.

The RFP part 2 says all seven companies must submit prototypes, at their cost. They have up to two months. The Brazilian Finance Ministry (Cory an' Gracia of course) will compare the quality an' consistency of the seven bids an' choose two successful bidders with whom the ministry will then sign a five year bulk contract for not just the 100 reals, but also the 1, 5, 10 an' 50. Big money for the winning company. Consistency, says the RFP, is key. So, each bidder must supply at least 5,000 blanks, an' not more than 15,000.

The classic confidence scam, don't appear overeager.

Cory doesn't ask for 15,000 blanks from each company. Not outright anyhows. He knows the competitive spirit is going to kick in an' they'll give 15,000 anyway just to show they can.

Results of the bid will be confidential. Each company will know the results of its bid, but not of the competing companies' bids.

Genius again. The companies have no clue. Once they've delivered 15,000 blanks each to Cory at their cost, not one of them will see a contract. Each will believe another company has won. Cory will repackage the 105,000 blanks, ship them to the US, an' overprint them as Uncle Sam's $100 bills.

Don't know how he got caught. He was doing real well for a while. Tells me, Gracia is living good 'til he gets out, an' then he has a few million stashed away, jus' waiting.

The problem is can he be patient until he gets out? Will she be patient? A guy like Cory, a million new schemes flittin' through his mind evr'y day, it's hard for him to qualify for good behaviour an' early release. He says to me: "Pango, I'm not getting younger here. Each day I sit here sees opportunities and life drifting away. I don't want to get out when I'm too old to enjoy life".

He doesn't say, but I know, Gracia is visiting less frequently an' he don't always look happy after the visits. She's mid-thirties, best I can tell.

Prob'ly doing those calculations that women do at that time of life. Putting the pressure on herself. Putting the pressure on Cory too. She wants children. It's now or never Cory.

Ifn' I was to bet on his patience, I wouldn't.

8. Henry or Hieronymus

I'm saying Hieronymus arrives on a Friday, looking like he's ready to cough up both his lungs. Pale as a vampire at the beach.

On paper his name is Henry Bosch.

In any other correction facility he'd be "Hank" or even "Heinrich" or "Heini". But at Dildo he's "Hieronymus". Sometimes "Mouse", sometimes "Ronny", an' finally "Hiero".

In the normal way of things none of us cons would know about Hieronymus. I mean the original. The painter guy who lived in the 1400s. Dutch. An' I'd like to know what he was smoking. Don't want any of it, 'cause judging from the way his paintings look, it gives him nightmares. The kind of thing you'd get maybe ifn' you mixed LSD with a triple dose laxative an' some dish soap to help you throw up.

Most cons are primary school or high school dropouts. A fair number are missing a few brain circuits as well. Lot of poverty, slow thinkers, eyesight problems, a few delusionals, hearing problems, some fetal alcohol symptoms, an' such. Your well-to-do educated man doesn't get into crime. Ifn' he does – because he's a politician or a white collar fraudster - he's rich enough to have a good lawyer. But at Dildo Correctional, everyone knows about Hieronymus Bosh, the painter.

See, Dildo has this waste of human space from the prehistoric tar-ponds of the gene pool. Franklin X. Wambaugh, prison psychologist an' a legend in his own mind. I heard once the X stands for Xavier. But the label on his door just says Franklin X. Wambaugh. He sees each of us about once a year. More ifn' we exhibit what he calls troubling personality disorders.

During a 15 minute session he decides ifn' we need any special treatment. The answer is: No, siree. Treatment costs tax-payer money. Franklin gets bonused for keeping the treatment budget low. His job is to protect the tax-paying public. So he prescribes exercise an' fresh air, or bouts of penitential reflection, self-awareness exercises an' a low calorie diet.

In Dildo Correctional, additional exercise an' fresh air means an additional tour of farm labour, or maybe the gravel pit.

Penitential reflection, self-awareness exercises an' low calorie means solitary confinement an' a reduced diet.

Even so, some cons look forward to the yearly pow-wow with Franklin X., the legend in his own mind. It's a half day off work an' maybe the ability to lead him up or down whatever garden path we can hook him on. Kind of like a once-a-year fishing vacation. See ifn' we can hook the big one.

Franklin tells us he follows the Freudian school of psychology. That's a fancy way of saying Franklin wants to hear about our sex lives, past, present, future, an' even in dreams. Ifn' you get him going on that subject you can get invited back for several days of discussion, again with no work. Extended trout fishing. When he's really hooked on whatever story you bait your hook with, he bites his nails.

There's a competition amongst long-timers at Dildo to see who can get him to bite his nails down the most an' who gets invited back the most days in a row. Each day with Franklin is another day off work.

One of Franklin's tests is to show us pictures an' ask

us to talk about the picture.

Be frank - he says – there are no wrong answers, say the first thing that comes to your mind.

One of his pictures is a painting by Hieronymus Bosh, titled "The Crucifixion of St. Julia". The title is real small, just about hidden, so most cons are confused by the picture. Little Joey, the first time he sees it, says. "Jesus got boobs? I think I'm getting religion."

Point is, at Dildo Correctional, everyone knows about Hieronymus Bosch the painter man. So when Henry Bosch the convict man arrives, natch he becomes "Hieronymus". An' that makes him a bit special for us cons at Dildo, our own Hieronymus Bosch.

An' the way he looks when he arrives, like he been through the combine an' spat out the other side with the chaff, I wouldn't be surprised ifn' he's on LSD, triple laxatives an' a side of arsenic too, just like the original.

9. Polite Conversation with Jeb

Dildo Correctional is a different. It gets federal funding ifn' it desegregates. The Warden likes money, no matter where it comes from so desegregation it is. He likes to be called "progressive". White, Black, Yellow, Brown, Red are mixed throughout the day. The guards enforce it. The hold-outs get some lumps from the guards until they keep their opinions to themselves. The Warden likes that too – shows he has complete control over his cons. His policies rule. Over every white-supremacist an' over every black power activist. Makes him stand out in the state as well. There's always lots of discussion about his policies, for an' against, but for sure everyone knows his name. Likes that too.

Part of life at Dildo Correctional is being assigned to work on Hoover's farm. Old Man Hoover pays the prison for our labour. Prison keeps most. Rumour says the Warden personally keeps another chunk. Still, us cons get a few coins put into our account too. Enough to buy a pack of smokes or two at the end of the week. We dig trenches to channel water into fields, or to drain swamps, or to turnover soil after harvest. Usually we're in long lines, shovels an' pick axes rising an' falling, sweating, an' digging. The guards are on foot watching. Sometimes in ATVs. Rifles ready. Zabriski comes with a dog on a leash, ugly looking brute straight out of a Bosch painting. The dog's no beauty either.

Now the dog isn't strictly part of prison pro-cee-dure, but Zabriski likes to bring it. Tells the Warden the cons have a special relation with it.

Which is true, we loathe it an' it loathes us. Ifn' it

weren't for the leash it would be at our throats, hamstrings or testicles.

Shortly after Hieronymus arrives I'm working a shovel in line next to Jeb. At Dildo Correctional we get allowed to speak quietly. Not that Jeb speaks much. But that day he looks at me. The whites of his eyes are red like he's spent too much time smoking bad weed.

He says - Pango, you got kids?

Uhuh.

How many?

I say - boy an' girl both grown up an' married. Doing OK. Proud of them.

He says – you're a con. They speak to you?

I say – they're over that. We speak, them an' me.

He gives me a look I can't figger.

I say - Jeb, you got kids?

He says - Mind your fuckin' business.

We go back to digging an' that's all he says to me that day.

10. Matthew

I said already as Zabriski's an ugly looking brute. We got an old-timer from the Deep South in the chain gang. Name of Matthew. We call him The Poet of Dildo. He talks real flowery.

Makes us cons smile.

He says to us, about Zabriski - if I had a dog that ugly I'd shave his butt an' make him walk backwards.

11. Math Interlude

Dildo Correctional offers a bunch of courses to cons. To better prepare them for re-in-te-gra-tion to the world out there. For cons who never finished high school, some of the courses come with teachers. These are civilians that come in, afternoons, weekday nights, an' weekends to help cons with their courses.

In my third year at Dildo there was a math high school class that went sideways one Sunday night. There was this real serious civilian math teacher explaining math inequality symbols. You know. A is less than or equal to B. A is strictly less than B. He's drawing the symbols like a megaphone or a megaphone with a line underneath on the blackboard to show the class.

Had a guy in the back of the class at the time, brother by the name of Low Dog. Real smart fellow, even though he has no high school. Guess he's bored with the class an' decides to have fun with the serious civilian. So Low Dog puts up his hand. Wants to ask a question he says, but it's all window dressing for what Low Dog really wants. The civilian doesn't know Low Dog from a hole in the wall. Doesn't know how tack sharp this guy is. Thinks it's a real question. Yes? He says.

Sir – says Dog, real polite at first – I seen you drive in here in a mighty fine Lexus SUV. You own that?

Yes - says the civilian, not sure where this is going.

Dog says -prob'ly you own a real nice house too. Now I never owned nothin' like that, nor my parents, nor their parents. An' as a convicted prisoner, ain't no one got less rights than me. I ain't even got the right to vote. Did you know that, Sir? We can't vote no how. How come you got the brass to come in here and lecture me on inequality? I know more about inequality than you ever will. An' what's this about less than OR equal? Like it's some wonderful choice and we should be happy with either option. That's just politician speak to make us feel good about being down-trodden. But we never goin' to be allowed to be equal, unless we demand it. Hell, I'm tired of less than. I don't want to hear less than, I don't want to be offered less than OR equal, like if I can't have equal then less than is good enough. I demand full equality. Why don't you teach us about equality?

By now half the audience is jumping up an' down demanding equality. The slow ones think it's for real an' the rest are just enjoying the break from a boring math lesson. There's a neo-Nazi lunatic con in the middle shouting about his equal rights. Why can't he have segregation in prisons? Why does he have to live with this riff-raff mix of sub-human races all day, every day? It's an insult to his god-given superior genes. He has a right to segregated math classes.

The civilian is totally stumped by all of this. Doesn't know what to say. The guards have to jump on it real quick. Have to settle things before it becomes a full riot or even a race riot. They're on their walkie-talkies to control an' it got this close to them bringing in the armed special response team to settle things an' bang heads.

Prob'ly the first time anywhere in the world that a high school math class nearly had armed response called in to break up a riot.

12. Aftermath

Low Dog an' the neo-Nazi got pulled out an' put in solitary confinement for 10 days each.

Low Dog said solitary was less boring than the math class, suited him jus' fine. Didn' want to go back to the math class.

The lunatic neo-Nazi said he was pleased too, said at least solitary is segregated.

13. Aftermath II

After he came out of solitary Low Dog gets told to do his yearly fifteen minutes with Franklin X. Wambaugh, prison psychologist an' legend in his own mind.

Low Dog spins Franklin yarns for four days straight. The kind that Franklin wants to hear. Keeps asking Low Dog back to explore further.

Seems Low Dog tells Franklin how he was a gardener for the Convent of Carmelite Nuns. In St. Louis, Missouri. After a big recruitment drive for young nuns-to-be. Tells how he's the only man in the convent, except for the priest who came to hear confessions, once a month. Low Dog tells he lasted two months because the priest was sick an' missed one month's confession. Claims if it wasn't for four of the nuns who confessed 'bout him end of the second month, he'd still be there. Low Dog shakes his head. Shame they couldn't keep quiet like the other five.

Franklin barely had fingernails after that session.

14. Alberta, Alberta

I spent a good few years working tramp steamers. Traveled the world's waterfronts, good an' bad, mostly bad. Picked up bit of this an' that language, which is why I can talk about Rio an' Brasilia with Cory an' say Ministério da Fazenda like a native speaker.

I get by in French, worked enough Japanese container ships that I get by in Japanese, I'm pretty fluent in German from working out of Bremerhaven for a few years. Good ships there, but got a bad German steamer one time in Singapore. Hard to believe, it was still coal-driven. When one of the stokers got sick from the heat I took on his job for a spell. Now there's a foul a job as ever bit a sailor in the rear. Don't know what kind of foul coal they were using. The coal dust gave me a cough that I still have.

Also, found out just how good the German language is for threats an' swearing. An' why some sailor's songs give over so much time to stokers:

In des Bunkers tiefsten Gründen,
Zwischen Kohlen ganz versteckt,
Pennt der allerfaulste Stoker,
Bis der Obermaat ihn weckt.

„Komm mal rauf, mein Herzensjunge,
Komm mal rauf, du altes Schwein,
Nicht mal Kohlen kannst du trimmen
Und ein Heizer willst du sein?"

Und er haut ihm vor'n Dassel,
Daß er in die Kohlen fällt
Und die heilgen zwölf Apostel
Für 'ne Räuberbande hält.

Und im Heizraum bei einer Hitze
Von fast über fünfzig Grad
Muß der Stoker feste schwitzen
Und im Luftschacht sitzt der Maat.

That's a real ugly song about a stoker working in 120F heat. An' having to put up with a Zabriski type brute of a first mate.

Scandinavian ships are best, they treat the crew good. Equipment is top notch. Ships under what sailors call flags of convenience, Liberia, Comoros, Togo, an' the like are crap, treat the crew like dirt, an' their ships are rust buckets. Liable to sink under the slightest gale. Got myself into a lot of trouble under flags of convenience.

Take the older days of shipping though. Before steam. Crew used to work together to raise this heavy anchor on a hundred foot of heavier chain, or raise several hundred pounds of canvas sails, pulling an' sweating on the ropes. They'd develop a rhythm so as to pull at the same time. No point one man pulling at a time. Those chains an' canvases can't be pulled that way. Have to pull together. In the navy, no talking allowed, nor singing, but sometimes they have a piper to give them the stamp an' go beat as they pull on the chains. Never heard one of the original tunes. These days so-called sea-chanteys is so sugared that you can't hear work in them. Might as well be an ad for deodorant.

Now-a-days ifn' you want to hear the real sweat an' strain in a work song, you need to hear a prison gang sing. It's raw like uncut rot-gut. Stings the eyes an' kicks you in the stomach. No way you can hear a prison gang without feeling that. Ifn' you never heard it before, makes you cry. Different prisons is different, at Dildo Correctional the farm gangs sing as we swing the picks an' shovels. The guards encourage it. Get us into the work tempo. Encourage us to pick up the beat an' sing faster. Our favourite is Alberta, Alberta. Also Rosie, an' Old Alabama.

Listen to that rhythm. First off it's sung real slow – every word slow with pauses like this

> 'Ber - ta 'Ber - ta

So that you can swing a heavy pick-axe in time. Then you got leave time for the aftershock when the axe bites the earth. Muscle an' bone shake an' then breathe.

> *Ber-ta in Meridian she – UHH PAUSE –*
> *living at ease oh-ah – UHH PAUSE*
> *Ber-ta in Meridian she – UHH PAUSE –*
> *living at ease well now – UHH PAUSE*
> *I'm on old Parchman, got to – UHH PAUSE-*
> *work or leave oh-ah – UHH PAUSE*
> *I'm on old Parchman, got to –UHH PAUSE-*
> *work or leave well now – UHH PAUSE*

Parchman farm, that's Mississippi State Prison farm. Guess they sing there too.

Here's how it goes:

O Lord Berta Berta O Lord gal oh-ah
O Lord Berta Berta O Lord gal well

Go 'head marry don't you wait on me oh-ah
Go 'head marry don't you wait on me well now
Might not want you when I go free oh-ah
Might not want you when I go free well now

O Lord Berta Berta O Lord gal oh-ah
O Lord Berta Berta O Lord gal well now

Raise them up higher, let them drop on down oh-ah
Raise them up higher, let them drop on down well now
Don't know the difference when the sun go down oh-ah
Don't know the difference when the sun go down well now

Berta in Meridian and she living at ease oh-ah
Berta in Meridian and she living at ease well now
I'm on old Parchman, got to work or leave oh-ah
I'm on old Parchman, got to work or leave well now

O Lord Berta Berta O Lord gal oh-ah
O Lord Berta Berta O Lord gal well now

When you marry, don't marry no farming man oh-ah
When you marry, don't marry no farming man well now
Everyday Monday, hoe handle in your hand oh-ah

Everyday Monday, hoe handle in your hand well now

When you marry, marry a railroad man oh-ah
When you marry, marry a railroad man well now
Everyday Sunday, dollar in your hand oh-ah
Everyday Sunday, dollar in your hand well now

O Lord Berta Berta O Lord gal oh-ah
O Lord Berta Berta O Lord gal well

Kept us going on many a day after we thought we couldn't. We got good at it. Sounded good. Got proud of how we sung it out loud. Proud of how we could swing the pick high an' hard. Kind of a secret defiance to the guards, to Zabriski, to the rifles an' that dog. Like saying, do your worst, I'm tougher than you'll ever be, I still have spirit to sing. There's still something living inside me. Not many things left for a con to be proud about.

15. Jeb Don't Sing

One of the few prisoners that won't sing is Jeb. Never hear the man sing a word. Just grunts. Zabriski tried to make a thing of it one time. Finally realized he'd look pretty silly putting Jeb on charge for disobeying an order to sing.

What's a legitimate order that a guard can give to a con is a grey area. An order to sing ain't it.

Still Zabriski wasn't happy at having to back down to a con. It's a control thing. Guards are all about control. A con who wins a control pissing match with a guard today is going to have trouble with the guard the next day. An' ifn' it ain't the next day, it'll be the next week, or the next month. An' ifn' it ain't the next month, it'll still come. The guard won't forget. Least of all Zabriski.

16. Romance

Zabriski's a pig. Still, some guards are better than others. Most of the cons get a smile out of young Sanderson.

One time he took us out to Hoover's Farm on a work detail an' said – boys, good news and bad news. First the good news. This morning you only need to work half a day.

We cheered.

Then he said – now the bad news. This afternoon you need to work another half day.

The guys who are slow on the uptake got angry. 'Specially Big Lenny, thought he was being ripped off somehow. Still most of us got a chuckle out of it.

I already told you, from my dorm window, I get a small view of the parking lot where the prison staff park. I can see the corner where Sanderson's pick-up is parked. It's a beat up old Ford. Real dusty. Noticed one day he gave Valerie a ride at the end of the day. Ifn' I do my usual trick there, stand on my toes an' angle my view through the cell window I can see Sanderson opening the passenger door for her to climb in. They both looked very serious, like it was a formal occasion, like they were young kids wearing formal clothes the first time ever.

The next day, I look out an' see that the Ford is all washed down an' cleaned up. An' Valerie has a new hair style two days later. From that day on I watch each day at the same time. After a month, I notice that Sanderson, puts his left hand on her arm to guide her into the passenger seat while he holds the door open for her with his right. An' Valerie gives him a thank-you smile as she slides into the seat. She's looking happier again, like in the days when her dick-head husband used to drop her off in the mornings. Smiles a lot.

I also get to understand some of the guards don't like Zabriski either. Should have guessed earlier. Thing is, in front of the cons the guards always seem like one mind. 'Cause one day Valerie's in the parking lot ahead of Sanderson. She's waiting for him. Zabriski rolls up in his pick-up an' waves for her to climb in, like he's offering to give her a ride. She shakes her head. 'Bout then, Sanderson walks up. Valerie backs away from Zabriski. Stands next to Sanderson, holding onto Sanderson's arm. Zabriski an' Sanderson have some kind of exchange that I can't hear. Valerie looks pale, Zabriski gets red in the face, then spits on the ground from his truck window an' roars off tyres screeching. Sanderson looks like he's comforting Valerie. Patting her arm, an' shaking his head at something as he watches Zabriski's tail lights. She leans against him, then smiles at him.

Then they go through the usual routine of him opening her door an' guiding her into the passenger seat.

17. Pro-ce-dure

Different jails do it different. Different states do it different. Federal an' state jails are different again. This is how it works in Dildo Correctional:

Guards that work inside Dildo on a daily basis, don't carry guns. Maybe a billy club. Maybe not. But no guns. Don't want cons overpowering a guard an' taking his firearm. Guards do carry walky-talkies. They can call for back-up, or they can call for the SRT, the special response team.

That's when a whole platoon load of armed guards drops on you carrying everything from Tasers to thunderflashes to tear gas to shotguns an' pistols. You don't want that, 'cause everyone – cons an' SRT are on edge when that happens. Ifn' a con next to you does something stupid, you're caught up in a mess of bullets, pepper spray an' flying billy clubs, whether you like it or no.

When cons go out of the prison, like going to work at Hoover's, they're tied up with chain to each other. They're a chain gang.

How that works is they line up in two columns. One next to the other. Each con is standing 'bout six foot behind the next guy in his column. Guards put down a line of chain next to each column. The cons put a loop of chain around their left ankle. The guards walk down each column, tighten the ankle loop an' close it round the cons ankle with a padlock.

Actually it's not a loop of chain around the ankles, it's more like the cons make a horseshoe shape with the chain around their ankles. The padlock squeezes tight the open end of the horseshoe an' locks it closed, ifn' you picture what I'm saying.

The cons now shuffle closer to the lead guy of each column. There's now maybe only three foot between each con in the column. Each con takes up the chain slack in his left hand. Now they get marched out, military style, lef-right, lef-right-lef, to the prison bus that's taking them to the farm. They file in from the front until the lead guy reaches the back of the bus. Then they turn, face forward, an' sit. One column sits on the right hand side benches, one column on the left. That's why you have two columns, each with its own chain.

Now, guards got to ride at the front of the bus with two chain gangs. They don't want 40 cons getting up during the ride an' coming forward. So, they padlock the front guy's chain to his bench, an' the back guy's chain to his bench. Now ifn' the guard's real careful, he'll lock the chain again at two, three, four or more benches down the length of the bus. That still leaves slack for some cons to move forward, but not so far now.

Hate to think what'd ever happen ifn' the bus crashes and takes fire. Can't imagine any guards walking back into the burning bus to unlock the chains from the bus benches. Makes me think of those ol' Roman galleys with prisoners chained to their oars. Don't suppose any soldiers thought of them when a ship sank.

Maybe tossed a key into the waves as the ship went under an' said – there's your key boys. Sort it out for yourselves ifn' you find it.

Meanwhile a separate bus has brought guards armed with rifles. Have to travel separately because procedure says no rifles within reach of the cons, on the bus or elsewhere.

That bus is supposed to follow immediately behind

us. When we get to Hoover's farm cons can't get out of their bus until the armed guards first take up position.

Thing is the armed guards bus is always late. The guards like to stop to pick up coffee an' donuts an' the like. So us cons sit in our tin bus at Hoover's an' bake in the heat like biscuits while we wait.

Matthew says it hotter than a goats butt in a pepper patch.

At Dildo the rest of us cons call it diesel therapy. Don't know what the diesel therapy is supposed to cure. Sweats the weight off you for sure. Not that many of us have a weight problem at Dildo.

Once the armed guards finally show up, the guards unlock the chains from the benches. 'Course the chains are still around the chain gang's ankles.

Now the cons march off to whatever field or swamp they're working on an' the armed guards follow. Armed guards stay back where no con can reach their rifles. Unarmed guards, the ones that were on the buses with the cons are in closer. The cons can get at the unarmed guards, but the rifles are still pointing at them from out of reach, an' from every angle, so what's the use.

At the end of the day, when the cons get back to Dildo, they again line up an' the guard takes off the ankle padlocks. All padlocks work off just one key, otherwise there'd be no end of messing about.

Pro-ce-dure says it's the guard that's supposed to unlock the chain gang. But some guards are plain lazy. They give the key to the con at the end of the chain an' say – unlock your own ankle, then walk forward, unlock every ankle on the chain, one at a time, then bring me back the key.

Saw Zabriski tell Cory one time to unlock a whole

chain. Thing is, Zabriski didn't see, but I did, Cory had a small piece of soap in his hand. Made me real nervous after that to be on a chain gang with Cory.

18. The Library

Many cons are primary or high school drop outs. Same is true for many guards. Ifn' you got a medical degree from Harvard you don't often become a prison guard. Result is, some of the clerical jobs with books an' files an' writing are done by civilians.

The library at Dildo Correctional is Mrs. Haverman. She's worked there 'bout 15 years. Course she gets convict help. I'm a helper some days. Which is why I can get to "The Child's Book of Victorian Parlour Games", 1878-1888, Volume 3, By Edgar G. Greenlock, without having to ask Mrs. Haverman, or some con to get it for me.

Mrs. H has gotten to trust me a fair bit. After a few years she starts to talk to me about her family. It's a thing of trust. Feels good to be trusted by someone in prison, 'specially someone who's not a con. Like they're saying you're a real person again.

At the same time, I'm not sure I want to hear what she's telling. She tells me that her mother is frail but still lives alone.

I say – Mam, that's not the kind of thing you should ever tell a prisoner. Please, Mam. Not ever. What ifn' some con marks your Mom as an easy target for when he gets out. Break into her house an' looks for cash an' stuff. Old woman, frail, all alone.

Mrs. H, she looks at me carefully, takes her time, an' says – I know you better than you think, Pango. As long as you keep it to yourself I've no worries about that.

I tell her I'll keep it to myself. An' I do.

She worries about her Mom an' we talk about that.

Also, her daughter, Julia, has moved out to college. Lives in residence at the college. Had to get a little car of her own now that she's no longer home with her Ma. Still can't decide between a career in music or chemistry. Switched back to music after two years of college chemistry.

Also in the library, I get access to the computer terminal, something most cons don't ever get. See, we use it for filing books, but I can also get to the internet.

Dildo Correctional doesn't like cons to have internet. Neither from a terminal nor from cell phones. 'Cause internet lets you have uncensored communication with the outside world.

Cell phones used to be a hot item for smuggling. That's over now. Having a smuggled cell phone don't do anything for you. Dildo Correctional has a broadcasting gadget that blocks cell phone calls an' internet.

Our communications with outside are supposed to be monitored an' censored. Don't want a con running a crime ring from inside Dildo Correctional, or writing to the New York Times to complain about the quality of the Friday night beans an' rice in the canteen, or organizing friends to break him out.

Some weeks ifn' I write my daughter a letter – normal paper letter with a stamp - something like "Next week I'll be on farm detail at Hoover's". She'll get the letter from the prison censor so heavily blacked out it'll say "Next ■■■■■ I'll be■■■■■■■■."

That's so she don't rent a helicopter gang with machine guns next week to bust me out of Hoover's farm. Fact that the censor takes a month to edit the letter, an' that it will arrive a month after I'm finished at Hoover's makes no whatever to the censor.

One time, she wrote back "Have fun when you're at

■■■■■■ next■■■■■■■".

Of course, the censors destroyed her letter without passing it on. Might have been a code that I'd worked out with my daughter. Censors have to be able to read all letters in plain English otherwise they get stopped.

But ifn' you help in the library an' file books an' the library is quiet you can do research for your divinity studies on the internet. Or you can look at pictures to remember what women look like. Don't do that a lot. Makes me sad.

Mrs. Haverman is also supposed to check what we're doing on the terminal an' review any browsing history. Her knees are bad with 'thritis though so she doesn't often walk over that way to check. An' I've learned to hide my browsing history. Mrs. H, she doesn't even know where to look for my browsing history. I've explained it to her once or twice when she asked, but her mind doesn't run to computers an' she's given up on that.

The guards don't check much on what I'm doing either. They come by an' see a book filing system an' they walk off again. The young guard, Sanderson, pays a bit more attention. I have to be careful when he's around.

One time he almost caught me or maybe he did – I'm not sure ifn' I was quick enough –looking at a photo of a young lady with a large smile and little else. Walked up behind me without me hearing him 'til the last moment. All he said was, "Divinity studies again, Pango? Concentrating on the latter-day saints and visions of the promised land?" an' then walked off.

Mrs. H. though, no problem for me to use the internet. She's strict in other ways though. Remember how I explained the "little lever" that confidence men like Cory use? All convicts try that on the civilian workers like Mrs. Haverman.

The way it works is you ask her to bring something really insignificant into the prison for you. The little lever. Maybe you ask for a bar of soap.

Mam, you say - prison soap is really dirty when you share it with other cons. I'd really like a bar of my own soap. For hygiene. Just a little bar? I don't want you to buy anything. Maybe you've got a leftover bar of hotel soap from the last Holiday Inn you stayed in? Even if it's part used that would be fine, Mam. Or if you have to buy it, I can give you the money from what I earn at Hoover's.

Ifn' she takes the bait, then she has broken all kinds of laws against smuggling contraband into the prison. That's a serious offence. An' ifn' she takes your money for the soap, it's bribery as well. Minimum is she'll lose her job ifn' it ever comes out, might lead to a criminal record or even jail time. Now that she's already broken the rules, she could be in trouble ifn' you ever squealed on her or let a guard find that soap. Now she owes you, she's yours, she's in so deep she can't refuse the next request.

You slowly up the ante, make the lever bigger an' bigger. Next it's sugar (for making moonshine), cigarettes, then it's matches you ask for, then a cell-phone, then take something OUT of the prison for me, Mam, maybe just a letter to my sister that the censor shouldn't see, it's a family matter, maybe there'll be a letter in return, an' so on up the scale.

Mrs. Haverman is wise to all that. It's part of the training that civilians at Dildo Correctional get from day one. Don't do favours for the convicts. They will up the ante. She's held out against that for all the years we work together. We like each other well enough, chat about this an' that, but no smuggling of even a little soap for me. So I still share soap with the others. But the internet in the library is mine.

19. Justice with a Side Order of Fries

Every prison has its share of jailhouse lawyers. Some cons get mighty good at legal proceedings and arguing cases. 'Cause they've been through the mill so often. Some, ifn' they can read an' have a leaning that way, spend time in the Dildo library boning up on the law. Maybe they've got an axe to grind on how they're being treated. Or how their case was handled. Or whether they should appeal. See prisons are required to provide a law library. By law. May sound odd to you. Or not. Comes out of an old 1997 court case called Bounds vs. Smith. So Dildo has a law library. Sounds grand when you say 'library'. More like a collection of books in the library. Not many books and not the easiest to figger out. Still an' all, there's usually one or two jailhouse lawyers working away at the books there, tryin' to figger out something or other.

After Hieronymus arrived, after we heard a bit about how he was convicted, I got curious. I don't use the law library though. I've looked at it once or twice an' then given up on it. Too hard to figger out. I'm not a jailhouse lawyer. Never will be. I don't know much about the legal proceedings. Only been through the courts one time. The time that put me here in Dildo Correctional. So what I did is I went to the internet an' I browsed our "convict scoreboard" in the library.

It's an internet scoreboard that a fair number of cons at Dildo like hear about from me. Kind of like following how your basketball team is doing week by week. It's run by some law schools out of Michigan an' California an' called The National Registry of Exonerations. Real fancy name. It lists near on 2000 convicts who've been exonerated over the last 25 or so years. Exonerated based on new evidence. Had their sentences overturned. After years in jail. About 16,000 years among all of them.

Now I told you I got an almost photo-graphic mem'ry. Here are some of the reasons for the wrongful convictions in that registry: false accusations, false confessions (we know how those happen), bad forensic evidence (happens a lot), inadequate legal defense (that means no money – only 24 states have a public defender system), official misconduct (that's where the judge an' prosecutor an' police ignore an' suppress evidence or offer reduced sentences to some lackey for making up evidence) an' lastly, no crime. That means someone is convicted where there was no crime.

Break your heart. It's all in that there registry.

Now ifn' you're new to the world of justice, you prob'ly asking how in heck can anybody be convicted for no crime. Our Hieronymus was. Here's a different case. Comes from another internet scoreboard I read up on an' tell the other cons about. It's an outfit called "Equal Justice Initiative", EJI.

It's a bunch of lawyers that goes around finding bad convictions an' overturning them. The Lone Ranger an' Tonto of the convicts' world. Every convict hopes someday they will ride into town an' free him – doesn't matter whether the con is guilty or not, he still dreams of that. Even our two neo-Nazi cons dream that, forgetting that EJI focusses on racial injustice and injustice for the marginalized.

Here's an EJI example of a no-crime conviction. I wrote it up in my diary word for word, but I know it by heart, my mem'ry doesn't throw stuff away, it just floats around in there:

"EJI won the release of Diane Tucker, an intellectually disabled woman who was wrongly convicted and sent to prison for a murder that never took place. Ms. Tucker and her sister, Victoria Banks, were convicted of killing a baby allegedly born to Ms. Banks, a baby she denied ever having. Medical evidence confirmed that Ms. Banks never had a child. Diane Tucker, Ms. Banks, and Ms. Banks' husband were convicted and imprisoned because their poverty and intellectual disabilities prevented them from defending themselves."

An' ifn' you think the legal system doesn't supress evidence, well here's another I wrote up in my diary. Comes from the National Registry of Exonerations. It's about a man called Carrillo in LA. Was exonerated after doing 19 years for murder. The Registry says:

"At Carrillo's sentencing, a criminal defense attorney came to court and told the judge that he represented a man who was at the murder scene and could testify that Carrillo was not involved, but the judge would not let him testify.

In March 2003, Carrillo, reviewing a defense investigator's files, discovered notes from the man who was not allowed to testify at his sentencing. According to the notes of the interview with the investigator, the man confessed to committing the shooting."

Don't want to recite everything that floats in my photo-graphic head, it goes on a bit an' then says:

"Ultimately, all of the eyewitnesses recanted at a post-trial hearing on a motion for a new trial for Carrillo. Turner

testified that Carrillo had been pointed out to him by the
police."

Prob'ly didn't help Carrillo that he's Hispanic, nor
that he was 15 when the shooting went down. You can
look up the cases for yourself ifn' you don't believe.
Anybody with an internet can find it. Just check the Equal
Justice Initiative and the Registry of Exonerations. It's all
written up in black an' white.

See, justice is like an assembly line for motor cars. The
guys don't get paid for stopping the line an' saying hey –
we gotto fix this gas tank on this here Pinto – there's a
problem here. They get paid for pushing through cars to
sell – more cars boys, more cars. Ifn' one guy stops or
slows down, he's letting down all his buddies on the line –
they can't work ifn' he's the bottleneck. They lose pay
ifn' he's the bottleneck. So problems have a habit of not
getting noticed. Schedules are more important.

The justice system is like that. Got a murder, find a
suspect, make your quota for crimes solved within two
weeks. Ifn' the suspect is poor, slow, don't speak real
well, don't understand well, can't afford a defence, an'
the jury don't like his skin, it'll be faster an' easier. Many
states the judge is an elected official. He won't get re-
elected ifn' suspects walk. An' he's on a schedule too. His
court docket is full to bursting. Ifn' he spends too much
time on any one case he'll never finish. OK boys, this is
the evidence we started with, this is what we roll with.
No eleventh hour evidence changes in my court room
else we'll never finish. This is fast food, not the Ritz. You
place your order, you pay, an' then no more changes to
your order. Keep those accused coming an' let's move 'em
through real quick. Another double hamburger with
fries, another car theft to convict, seen a million an' we

don't look closely at any of them anymore. Next.

20. An' Another Thing 'Bout Justice

An' one more thing about justice. We're all supposed to be equal in the eyes of the law. How come the court clerk says – All rise for Judge Smith - or whatever the judge's name is?

How come no-one ever says to the judge an' jury – All rise for the accused Abner Fast-Fingers Jones - or whatever his name is?

Don't sound real equal to me. Sounds more like that old time feudalism we used to learn about in school. The American Revolution was supposed to get rid of all that bowing an' scraping before nobles who you had to call "my lord" an' "your honour". Don't think the revolution has reached the court rooms yet.

21. The Innocent Con

I told you about The National Registry of Exonerations and EJI. Don't want you to think all us cons are innocent. The majority of us are guilty as hell, self included, no matter what they tell you. An' they'll tell you the craziest things.

They say – I'd be a free man today if my lawyer hadn't got his degree off the side of a Rice-Crispy box. I kept telling him what our defence strategy should be, an' he ignored me.

Or they say– I'd be a free man today if the Sheriff wasn't sleeping with my wife. They cooked this whole thing up to get me out of the way. How's an innocent man supposed to fight that with both the Sheriff and his wife testifying 'gainst him?

Another guy tells me the judge that put him away owes him $200,000 for a poker game.

Says - I had four aces and this judge bet the whole pot with only a full house. Threes and sevens. I hate to see a man bluff with such a bad hand. Sides which, judges are the worst poker players. I mean in real life when does a judge ever have to bluff? It's not like he has to bluff at sentencing any of us.

Hey, I'll see your two years with no chance of parole an' raise you another two?

An' who bets everything on threes and sevens? But hell, I wasn't going to let him win was I? Then he tells me he can't pay. So he decides to get rid of his debt by putting me in prison.

See if he puts me away long enough then the sta-tute of li-mi-tat-ions on his debts kick in before I'm a free man.

If he just told me he couldn't pay I'd've said - Forget it. No problem.

$200 thousand was pocket money for me when I was a free man. Wouldn't have given a damn if he couldn't pay. Heck, I used to buy a new boat every time my old one got wet.

I'd have said - George, my man, forget it. What's $200 thousand to a man like me? Buy me a rye an' coke an' we're quits. An' George, do me a favour, don't do that again. Doesn't look good on a judge, betting more than he can afford.

Now that I'm a con I've lost my business, my houses, my motor yacht down on the Florida Keys, my little chateau on the south coast of France, and my antique cars. $200 thousand is a lot of money now. Say, buddy, you got any tobacco?

'Casionally though we find a con who's innocence shines through like St. Julia on the cross. It's something us cons can recognize. We got the nose for it. Can smell it clearly, more clearly than any judge an' jury. Those cons are like a saint in our midst. They get treated a bit special by the others. Get some extra care an' sympathy.

Hieronymus' story came out slowly. When he arrived he had serious pneumonia. Got transferred to the prison hospital at Dildo the same week Jeb an' Howell both came down with something from ticks that bit them. Bit them both while they was working on draining a swamp at Hoover's. Jeb's leg swoll up like a balloon an' he ran a fever of 103. Howell's fever hit 102 an' he was throwing up like those diesel pumps the county uses for draining ditches. So the three of them are all cooped up in the same prison hospital ward. I got the story afterwards from Howell.

Turns out Hieronymus an' Jeb get on fine. Surprise to everyone, 'cause Jeb's never gotten on with anyone in his life. Seems Jeb has a hidden thing for playing chess. Is actually good at it. He an' Hieronymus take time in the hospital playing 'gainst each other. They're both good. An' they start talking while they play. They ignore Howell. He's kind of invisible 'because he's ancient an' never speaks anyway.

'Cept to say – pass the bucket, I'm going to throw up.

So I learn a bit more about Jeb from what Howell overhears. Jeb's got a 22 year old daughter who won't speak or write to him, 'cause he's a con. It's eating him up every day. She started going out steady with a young guy from a good family. She thinks having a dad who's a con will get in the way of that.

An' I get to hear about Hiero.

Hiero's from Minnesota. They speak different than us Southern folk. That's part of what got him into prison. He's also a fish – one of those innocent people who have no sense of the dangers around them. Ifn' you put a bear trap in front of him, an' a sign saying – BEAR TRAP – in big letters, he'd say - wonder what that is? He'd walk right in then act surprised when the jaws clamp tight onto his leg. He'd argue how wrong that was. He'd say – hey that sign is wrong. I'm not a bear. This thing is dangerous to HUMANS. Why didn't the sign say?

There are people like that. No street smarts. Smart in terms of education, but a danger to themselves every time they cross the street. Just innocence.

He studied to be a history teacher. Didn't leave him barely any money after he got his degree so he applies for the first job that he can see – down South. He flies down for the interview on his almost last dime. They tell him they'll let him know. He goes back to the airport for his return flight to Minnesota. He's reading a newspaper. He's bored. So he starts singing to himself there in the airport waiting room. He likes old-style gospel. Got a good voice. Sings in a choir back home. There in the airport he sings quietly to himself "No-one knows the troubles I've seen". Talk about prophecy. Should of sung "No-one know the troubles I'm gonna see". Anyways. Then he reads a bit more. Then he sings "There is a balm in Gilead". He's a bit louder now, 'cause he's forgotten about the rest of the world. The innocent fish doesn't realize the way Southerners speak is 'bout to get him into a mess of trouble.

Three guys sitting near him get up an' fetch security. The police come running. They drag him into the airport cop shop, real quick. They're in a hurry. There's lives at stake. They've already stopped the loading of the Hiero's plane. The luggage on the plane is being inspected by sniffer dogs. The flight is cancelled. The bags waiting to be loaded have been frozen – no further movement until they're inspected. The waiting room where Hiero was sitting is being evacuated. Where is the bomb they say to him? We've got three witnesses they say. Where is the bomb?

Hiero doesn't understand the Southern accent. He answers the question the way he hears it. He says, poor fish – in Gilead.

The cops do some quick research. Seems there's one Gilead that's a giant bio-pharma company, a Gilead town in Maine, an' a Gilead village in Oklahoma. This is getting beyond the reach of the local cops. They escalate while the baggage search continues. As far as they're concerned Hiero's being un-co-operative. They keep pounding the same question – where is the bomb?

An' all he can reply is either –in Gilead – or even

worse – in the trees.

That's clearly a stalling tactic. An' that innocent fish expression he gives them is drivin' them wild. The cops are getting angrier every minute.

Worst of all sometimes when they say – where's the bomb? he says – on the wounded.

Within 10 minutes of their escalation five HUGE black SUVs pull up, got those little wireless communication aerials sticking up all over them like half-bald porcupigs, an' Hiero is handed over to a new branch of security. Feds of some kind. Hiero isn't clear whether they're FBI or CIA or what, but he's now an item of national security. With national security at stake these new guys don't care what they have to do to get answers.

Sitting there playing chess with Jeb an' handing the bucket to Howell, Hiero is still scared to talk about what they did to him. My guess, an' it would explain his pneumonia an' water in his lungs, is these fine protectors of our democracy waterboarded him.

When they finally got to the point where they understood the issue was a language issue of bomb vs balm – both pronounced the same down South – they had a major embarrassment on their hands. Something that they needed to cover up.

They made clear to him he had two options – admit to a bomb hoax an' get treatment for his lungs or face more questioning. He was coughing so badly he couldn't even speak – just signed. One more thing, they said, everything you've seen and heard while with us is confidential – it's a matter of national security – you will never speak of this to anyone, under pain of imprisonment on treason charges, sign here. He coughed an' signed. Then the security guys handed him back to the local cops with the signed confession of a bomb hoax.

With no money left for any kind of defence lawyer, Hiero tried to defend himself in court. His southern judge couldn't hear the difference between bomb an' balm, no more'n the airport police could. The judge became so angry with Hiero's rambling, coughing, defence – I said bal – cough -m not bo – cough -mb - that he shut down Hiero's defence after barely two minutes. Why listen to this drivel when the signed confession was at hand. Case closed. Sentenced to three years at Dildo. Next case.

'An ifn' you remember the reasons the National Exoneration Registry gave for wrongful convictions, well St. Hiero the innocent fish matches 5 of the 6:

False accusations, false confessions, bad forensic evidence, inadequate legal defense, official misconduct, and no crime.

22. Matthew II

Talked to Matthew, The Poet of Dildo, one time about the neo-Nazi an' his segregated solitary. Matthew didn't say much. Spat an' said only - dumber than a tick on a dead dog, that one.

Matthew spent a fair bit of time with Hieronymus. Trying to educate him on how folk talk in the South. Said – listen up Hiero. You gotta unnerstan' the way we talk down here.

Fr'instance up North when you folk tell fairy tales, you say

"Once upon a time...

In a land far, far away...

There lived a poor fisherman and his wife.

He wasn't very smart and she wasn't very nice. Still, they were happy."

Right?

Now that ain't no way to tell a good story. Down here nobody gonna unnerstan' that. This is how you tell it. What you say is:

"Y'all not gonna believe this sheeyit.

This here thing happened up in Boston.

There was this fisherman an' his wife. Didn't have a pot to piss in between them, nor a window to throw it out of. He wasn't the sharpest knife in the drawer. Half the time he didn't know whether to check his ass or scratch his watch. Not that he had one. On account of them being poor, too poor to paint, too proud to whitewash. Now his wife, she was lower than a snake's belly in wagon rut. Stuck up too. Thought the sun rose jus' to hear her crow.

Don't know why he married her. But what with him being a fisherman an' all, maybe she had worms. Still, they were happier than a daid peeyig in the sunshine."

There, Hiero, think you can say it the way we say it? Daid peeyig?

Hiero says – dead pig.

Can't say it. Then he gets distracted with questions. Innocent fish that he is.

Matthew, why is a dead pig happy in the sunshine?

Matthew says – cause when the peeyig dries up in the sun, his lips shrink an' curl. Like a smile. You never been on a hawg farm, Hiero? Try it again, daid peeyig.

Hiero listened hard, but never did get the hang of Southern talk.

23. Schedules and Food

Life inside Dildo Correctional follows schedules. Cons get to so used to the schedules. They don't have to look at a watch to know them. A weekday, depending on your dorm an' workday tasks, an' depending whether you're working in the prison or out, might look like this:

6:30am wake up.

Now given that lights out in the evenings is real early, cons are awake anyway. Ifn' not there is a loud buzzer, accompanied by a recorded voice saying 6:30 am. The voice is nagging, loud and metallic. Would irritate the hell out of even a saint. You want to put your hands over your ears an' shout – Shut UPPPP.

'Til you get used to it. That genr'lly takes 'bout three years.

Now ifn' you're in a dorm of 'bout twenty other cons, no way you're going to stay asleep what with the buzzer, the bullhorn voice, an' the other cons griping an' shouting – Shut UPPP.

That buzzer an' bullhorn voice repeats throughout the day to tell you it's exercise time, or lunch break or whatever.

6:30 to 7:15am ablutions, ready bed and dorm for inspection

Cons don't have much kit for inspection. Still, beds must be ready, toothbrush, toothpaste an' towel laid out square on the bed frame, the dorm swept, an' the bathrooms cleaned. The guards set out a roster of who is responsible each week for sweeping an' bathrooms. Sweeping, by the by is kind of a pain. Dildo don't trust you with a full size broom. Might use the handle as a stick to beat on your guard. So you get a little brush with a tiny handle to do the sweeping. On your knees.

7:15 to 7:45am roll call, assignment of work teams for after breakfast, and inspection

7:45 to 8:15am exercise

These are carried out under the control of a guard on the gravel in front of the dorm.

8:15 to 9:15 breakfast

The same guard marches the cons in that dorm to the canteen for breakfast, then marches them back.

9:15 to noon

Assigned work teams. This might be farm detail, machine shop, gravel pit an' the like. Depending on the weather an' the assigned work, there'll usually be a 15 minute break at 10:45 for cigarettes an' water. Ifn' your guard likes to smoke, an' most do, you may get a few other smoke breaks.

Noon to 1pm

Roll call, lunch, either in the prison canteen or at the worksite.

1 to 2:30 pm

Continued work

2:30 to 3:00 Return to exercise yard, roll call.

3:00 to 4:00 Exercise or sports

4:00 to 5:30 School, studies, or library time

5:30 to 6pm Supper in canteen

6 to 7:30 Letter writing, reading, phone calls.

7:30 to 8:30 Rake gravel in front of dorm, ablutions, clean bathroom, evening inspection, evening roll-call.

8:30 Lights out.

Cons become ha-bit-u-ated to the schedule. You'd think we'd welcome any change in schedule. No siree, after a week or three cons learn - change is never good. Change is bad. Change means you an' your dorm are going to be searched, you'll lose tobacco, or matches, or those soaps you've carved into domino tiles. Change means the Special Response Team is coming to bang heads, or someone is being dragged off to solitary, maybe you. Or your dorm is gonna be given extra duties an' losing privileges because you or one of your dorm cons screwed up. Change means you'll be late for breakfast or lunch or supper. Means other dorms will finish any good food before you get there. Not that there ever is good food. But ifn' ever there was good food, an' you're late, it'll be gone.

Cons get anxious, it's getting late, maybe they'll miss breakfast entirely, or lunch, or supper. This is not the outside world where you can catch up on a missed meal by stopping in at your local burger joint on the way to work, or maybe take a late lunch because your meeting ran late.

After a month or two cons are so ha-bit-u-ated they NEED their meals on time. Delaying a con's meal is like ringing bells for those Russki dogs an' watching them howl an' drool over an empty bowl whenever they hear bells.

24. Cory's Choir

Whenever Cory starts in on something I wonder what his angle is. Genius like that, I know he's thinking twelve chess moves ahead. Trouble is I can barely think one move ahead. I never know what he's planning or what his real payoff will be.

After Hiero arrives, Cory starts on about having some of us cons form a Sunday night choir. I think I kicked off whatever scheme he's planning. Didn't mean to. We were talking about something else. Think he asked me what languages I speak. Told him. Then sang for him a few of those German verses about the stoker. He got this far away look.

Said to me – Pango, that's not bad. Did you know, Hiero used to be in a choir?

An' then started spouting about having our own choir.

He tells some of us he'll get us extra privileges or Sunday night, including ice-cream soft drinks an' cake from the Warden. He tells the Chaplain we'll work in a few religious numbers. For those of us that know Hiero's story, he says we'll perform Balm in Gilead in public one day. Might get someone to rethink Hiero's conviction. He tells others we might get good enough to get on a recording label. He tells about how Glen Sherley in California's Folsom Prison has written songs for Johnny Cash. To others he talks about getting access to guitars, drums, horns an' the like. Talks at us how the choir at Kansas' Lansing Correctional got to sing outside prison walls to a real people public. Tells us that some prison group in Malawi, somewhere the hell in Africa, has even been nominated for a Grammy. An' to all he talks about breaking the Sunday night boredom in the dorms.

While the cons are arguing about this idea, Cory starts in on the guards. Eventually Sanderson an' the Chaplain take the idea to the Warden, who says OK on a trial basis. We can use the prison chapel an' the piano in the chapel. Soft drinks an' cake is OK in limited quantities. That's big, because us cons never see enough sugar at Dildo. No guitars or other instruments for now. The Warden says – let's see. An' Cory has to limit the choir to a dozen singers for now.

That's how Cory's choir starts. For the most part he picks his dozen well. He makes one or two choices that I don't get. He insists that Rapid-Glen be part of the choir. Rapid-Glen is in for car theft. Rapid because he unlocks an' hotwires cars real quick. He can barely carry a tune in a bucket, an' has a wide mean streak in him that I could never cotton to. Don't know what Cory sees or hears in him. But for the rest – we actually sound pretty good.

Cory his'self does a great solo tenor. Hiero is a good alto solo. The rest of us are used to singing together an' pretty darn good back up. The first two Sundays are a success. We sing some songs from Hoover's Farm, try prison standards like Jailhouse Rock, try Take this Hammer to the Captain, an' even play with Eric Clapton's Sunshine of Your Love.

Another surprise is the piano. We thought maybe Hiero would play for us. He's not bad on the piano. Half an hour into the first Sunday, while he's mooching around the keys to figger out some tune that he doesn't yet know Slow Joey steps forward.

Says - It's like this.

Shows Hiero how to play it. Shows him the melody line, right hand, shows him the basic chords, left hand, puts both hands together.

Says - Add this if you want it to rock – do this if you want it to be slow – like this for gospel – like this for honky-tonk or blues.

Huh. Could have wiped the floor with the rest of us. Never heard a piano sound so good. Slow Joey. No-one thought he was good for anything much until that moment. Hiero gets up from the piano.

Says - SJ, from now on you're our pianist.

SJ looks surprised.

No – he says – you the pianist – I was just showing you the tune.

He has a bit of trouble saying all that. He stutters real bad 'cept when he sings.

Hiero says – No – we've just found a much better pianist. SJ you're it.

Turns out SJ is a piano gold. Ifn' you can hum it or sing it, he'll work out the piano part in five seconds flat. Makes no never mind ifn' he never heard the tune before. Never seen anything like it. An' he doesn't even know how special he is.

Soon became obvious though we need a choir master. Otherwise we're going spend all our time arguing about what to sing next an' whether it's even something a choir can sing. Just cause Little Joey's a Drake fan (whoever that is) doesn't mean it's choir music, or that anyone else in our team gives a damn to sing it. Without a choir master the Sunday choir is going to end very quickly.

Don't know how Cory saw this coming, but somehow he must have known. I had the answer.

25. Soap or Julia

On Tuesday morning I had library duty with Mrs. H. Gave me all of Monday to figger out my approach. What Cory would call the psy-cho-lo-gy of the deal.

I figgered I'd first ask for something that she'd turn down, then ask for what I really wanted. Maybe she'd feel bad about turning me down for my first ask. Be more prepared to say yes to the second.

Ifn' you think that's underhand, remember a con has limited options.

I was carrying a stack of books for her.

I said – Mrs. H, you ever give thought to bring me some soap?

She says – No, Pango, we've talked about that a million times.

I put on a sad face.

OK - I say - Can I ask you something else?

You can ask - she says.

I tell her about the choir, about how good SJ is at the piano, I sing a little bit of "Take this Hammer to the Captain", tell her Hiero's shaping up real well as an alto now that his pneumonia's gone, tell her about the enthusiasm among the dozen cons, an' two dozen more that didn't get picked in the trial phase.

Sounds real nice, Pango – she says- Might do a lot of good for some of the cons. What is it you want?

Mam – I say – we need a choir master.

Don't look at me – she says.

No, Mam - I say - I was wondering whether your daughter would volunteer. Julia. Just a couple of hours every Sunday night in the chapel. What with her being a music student again at college. Might even be good experience for her.

She says – I'll ask her, Pango. You back on library duty tomorrow morning?

Yes, Mam – I say - I'm very grateful.

She says – I'll let you know tomorrow.

An' that's how we got our choir master. Turned up the very next Sunday, jus' over five foot tall, would've drowned in a five foot two snow drift, but ran us like a chain gang from the moment she walked through the door.

26. Julia

Julia walks into the prison chapel. Sunday evening an' the dozen cons are already lined up. Waiting inside. Two guards escort her in. Sanderson, an' Venter. She steps forward an' says to us. Gentlemen, I'm Julia Haverman. If you can sing, I'm going to be your choirmaster.

The cons stare. We're stunned. She's early twenties, black hair, bright blue eyes. Barely more'n five foot tall. It's clear she's tried to dress down, no makeup, an' some baggy dress thing like a tent. Dark blue. Maybe it's meant to hide her figure, but its failing, big time. The moment she steps forward the tent drapes itself to show her curves. I'm looking at Chiefy. He's a short compact con, pushing well past sixty. One of the calmest guys in Dildo Correction. Nothing phases him. 'Cept now. His eyes are bulging, there's sweat on his cheeks. He's gulping like a gold fish at feeding time. Seems none of the cons are even breathing.

One exception, Little Joey, as usual, can't keep his big mouth shut.

Holy St. Julia on a cross – he says – Those boobs are as good as the painting. I got religion again.

Venter is on him instantly. Marches him out of the chapel. Sanderson stands against the side wall an' watches, he looks at Julia, like he's asking something. She shakes her head at him an' he leans back an' waits.

Julia steps forward again. She speaks low but clear. We can all hear.

She says – I heard you needed a choir master. Is that right?

The cons nod, an' mutter – yes Mam.

Ifn' you know the cons like I do you can hear they're embarrassed at Little Joey. They don't know rightly know what to say or do 'bout him. Me neither.

She says – I want you to be really clear on this. We're going to be really clear on this. If you're just looking for a woman to ogle, I'm not staying.

She pauses. We don't dare move.

Then she says - So, all those who want me to work with you as a choirmaster with a real choir move over to this side of the chapel.

She points to her left.

All those who just want to ogle me because I'm a woman, move over to this side. She points to her right.

We all move to her left, except Slow Joey. He's dead in the middle. Not left, not right.

She glares at him.

Make up your mind – she says – do you want to sing with me or stare at me?

SJ can't move. He's always slow at understanding. An' decisions. This time round I think he understands the choice, jus' he wants to do both an' he's too honest to hide it. The most honest con in all of Dildo Correctional. So he's choosing both. Right in the middle. But when she says do you just want to stare at me, he's embarrassed. Shuts his eyes to show he's not staring. At least, not right then.

Rightly speaking all of us would stand in the middle with SJ. We do want to ogle her, an' we want her to direct our choir, but we're embarrassed to stay in the middle.

I pull SJ over to her left.

I say – 'scuse him Mam, his name's Slow Joey. An' he means no disrespect. He's just slow some days.

She looks at him an' says – is that right Mr. Joey?

Joey, turns red with all the attention. I say for him – he stutters real bad Mam, 'cept when he sings, an' he's our pianist. Play anything for you. Better than any concert piano man.

She asks again – is that right Mr. Joey?

He nods.

Manages to say – I c-can p-play a bit.

Right – she says – move over to the piano Mr. Joey.

She puts some sheet music in front of him. Play – she says.

He's frozen. Looks panicked. Looks like he wants to cry. Says - I c'c'c'...

He can't get the words out. He looks at me.

Mam – I say – he doesn't read music or anything. He just plays. If you tell him a tune he knows he'll play. If you hum him a tune he doesn't know – he'll play.

She nods. OK – she says to me – what's the last song you all tried together?

I say – Mam, last week we had a go at "Take this Hammer".

She looks at Joey. Says – can you play it?

He nods.

She says – play it please.

He plays, kinda the way a child plays, learning the piece.

She looks at me. It's a question. Like she's saying what is this crap?

I say – Mam, he's wound up tight. If we can get Cory an' Hiero to sing with him, he'll play like a 10-piece orchestra.

She says to him – is that right Mr. Joey?

He stops playing, nods.

She looks at the others. She says – Mr. Cory an' Mr. Hiero? They step forward. She says - Can you start it off?

They look nervous too. Hiero says – Mam, could we all do this together – all eleven of us? We're used to doing this together.

She nods.

We gather round. Cory starts us off. We're sounding OK. An' Joey. Joey sounds like a goddam steam powered symphony orchestra.

Julia listens, she watches us, she's got a notebook open an' is taking notes. At the end of the song she says to us – Gents – I think we can turn you into something good. If you work.

We're all nodding. We're pleased.

Then Julia looks at Slow Joey.

She gives him a nod an' says – Mr. Joey, that was – she pauses an' Joey looks like he wants to shrivel up. 'Cause she's looking at him real serious. Then she says – Mr. Joey, that was amazing. No work needed where you're concerned. That's as good as it gets. An' for the first time that evening, she smiles.

Joey goes red in the face again an' doesn't know where to look.

An' funny thing, none of us question this youngster's right to judge Joey like that.

Then she looks back at us an' says again – you can be good, if you work. That means you show up every Sunday. Not one or two of you. Not nine or ten. All of you. If you can't do that you should walk out new. I'd rather work with six hard workers than with six who work and another six who sometimes don't. No hard feelings if you leave now.

She waits. None of us move.

So – she says – we're agreed on working?

Yes, Mam – we say.

Don't know where this young woman gets her steel. I watch the other cons. She's got us in the palm of her hand. All maybe except Rapid-Glen. He's got a calculating look on him which I can't figger.

Another thing – she says. So far I've heard you're doing this because you get soft drinks and cookies and break the Sunday boredom. You need a better reason for working hard. I need a better reason for working with you. The guards need a better reason for being here.

I'm going to give you that reason. In two months time we're performing for the other prisoners and for the guards, in four months' time, you're going to give a performance to outsiders. I'll sort out where and to whom and let you know. OK?

The cons look at her, open mouths. This thing has gotten a life of its own.

Yes, Mam – they say, like sleep walkers.

Don't know ifn' this was part of Cory's twelve move ahead chess game. Cory's face doesn't show anything. Then again, ifn' he's planning something, it won't.

The rest of the night she works on getting to know our names an' voices. She works us with singing exercises to figger out what our singing ranges are – meaning how high or low we can sing. Tells each of us we're countertenor, tenor, bass whatever. She works us through some standard songs with us singing what she calls unison – means we all sing the same melody.

Next time - she says - we'll start with exercises, then we'll move onto using your different ranges to offset each other's voices. Answer and response, fugues, canons, rounds. And we'll get some of you comfortable with solos too. We'll figure out what kind of songs you want to sing.

An' that's how we got a choir master.

27. A Poor Man's Made Out of Muscle and Blood

I heard this from Howell again. Howell being ancient an' harmless he often gets paired with Jeb for work assignments. That's why when Jeb gets tick bites, likely Howell's in the same swamp getting the same kind of tick bites an' landing up in the same hospital ward.

Even ifn' you're a violent case like Jeb, you're not likely going to beat on an old harmless guy like Howell. Anyhow, seems the two of them had been given duties on the Sunday night to wheel the full swill bins from behind the canteen to the back gate for the hog farm trucks to pick up.

They wheel the empty carts back to the kitchen just as our choir group is marched out of the chapel that first Sunday. Jeb don't pay much attention until Sanderson escorts out Miss Julia. When Jeb sees her he stops dead. Like he's turned into a salt column in Gomorrah. Howell is coming up behind him with another cart, runs his cart right into Jeb. Jeb doesn't even notice. He's staring at Miss Julia. The guard with them, man by the name of Harrison, tells Jeb to get moving. Jeb doesn't move. The guard is shouting now. Jeb doesn't move. Jeb only starts moving again when Miss Julia's out of sight.

The next Sunday, Jeb asks to be part of the choir. Being it's Jeb, it's more like he demands to be part of the choir. The guards don't care either way. With Little Joey gone, there's space for one more. Us cons are scratching our heads. None of us has ever heard Jeb sing. Heck, we barely hear him talk. The only thing I can remember him saying to me is the time he said - Mind your own fuckin' business.

Julia looks at him seriously, like she looks at all of us.

She says - I need to hear you sing something. What do you know?

Jeb shrugs. Says - you pick, Mam. – I'll tell you ifn' I know it.

I notice he's speakin' real gentle an' polite. Not the Jeb I know.

Julia tries this an' that. Jeb doesn't know the songs she's asking for. Keeps shaking his head. She changes course.

Says – Jeb, what work did you do before prison.

Mam – he says – I was a miner, hard-rock miner.

She looks up at this huge man, an' nods.

Thinks a moment an' says – do you know how to sing any mining songs?

Sure – says Jeb. How about I sing sixteen tons, Mam?

OK – she says. Mr. Joey can you follow along on the piano? Let Jeb set his own pace.

The rest of us are watching. Still kind of amazed.

Jeb shuts his eyes, his lips move quietly, like he's running through the words in his head to remember.

Then he takes a deep breath.

I'm expectin' him to start with - I was born one morning when the sun didn't shine.

Doesn't happen that way. Every single thing he does with that song is not what I'm expectin'. He starts –

I was born in the driving rain...

The sound shocks us all. It's loud. It's deep. It's got a tune to it an' a beat. His timing draws you in.

I was booooooooooooorn ...

Hangs on the word born. Draws it out 'til you think it's a mighty wind you're hearing, the same gale that's driving the rain. He draws out the word "rainnnnnnnnnnnnnnn" too. It goes on an' on. He's got big lungs.

Then the sound gets real interesting. Takes me a moment to realize why. Miss Julia is singing a high note. No word, just a high kind of harmony. Sounds real good. Then he changes the rhythm, picks up the pace an' he's singing to a faster beat. Joey's piano follows. Julia keeps up her harmony.

Some people say a man is made out of mud,
A poor man's made out of muscle and blood ...

The rest of us can't help it, we're quietly tappin' our shoes on the chapel floor an' humming along. Sounds real nice. Like a backup rhythm section.

He gets to the end of a "... with a mind that's weak and a back that's strong" an' glances at the rest of us to see ifn' anyone's going to dare call him on it. We don't. Just keep the beat an' our low hum goin'.

I'm no musician, never was, never will be, but his pauses when you didn't expect them, an' then how he keeps the melody going in spite of the pause, don' know how he did it. Also seems wrong that such a mean guy, can have such talent. Anyhows, song comes to an end an' he's got one more joker up his sleeve. His final line –

I owe my soul to the company store

He drags out oooooo-oooo-oooo-we an' his voice gets

83

lower an' deeper an' deeper. Never heard anything like it.

He stops an' we all clap.

Miss Julia is nodding. Says – that wasn't my favourite song - until now Jeb. You may just have changed that.

He looks at her real serious an' jus nods.

Finally says – Mam, am I in the choir?

She nods too. Says – you're in.

I'm thinking of it all that week – what are the chances of our choir having two such strong talents – both Mr. Joey, an' Jeb coming together in the same place. An' two cons at that. Guess it happens sometimes, like John Lennon meeting Paul McCartney, or Simon meeting Garfunkel. To have it happen to us bums, drifters, addicts, criminals an' mental cases seems mighty strange, like two bolts of lightning coming together.

28. Politics

Said Miss Julia works us like a chain gang. Works us hard. No excuses. We learn words, learn tunes by listening an' repeating – none of us read music. Sometimes seems our heads an' throats are bursting. Can feel ourselves getting better though. Every Sunday a bit better. Thinking of the songs during the week. Practising the words during the week.

The first show is inside Dildo. For the other cons, guards an' the civilians who work Dildo Correctional.

Cory, he takes Miss Julia aside. Says to her – Mam, you going to have a problem performing for a Bilbo Correctional audience.

She says – what kind of problem?

He says – No problem if the audience hates us. A big problem if the audience likes us.

She says – what?

Cory tries to explain.

It's politics. See some of our guards, they don't have much education, don't have good pay, don't own a fancy car or a fancy house, don't have much of a future other than this job, their kids might never get to college. The only thing so far that they can feel good about in life is that they get treated better than us. Got more status. Get to order us around. Get to control us.

How they going to feel if the see a mere convict on stage, under the bright lights, getting attention from a young woman choir master, getting treated like a little rock star? How they going to feel if the Warden and his wife are applauding, if the whole prison audience is applauding us?

Maybe you were planning to have the Warden to introduce us on stage. That would be bad. The Warden would be treating us like stars and ignoring the guards. Hell, if the concert's good, the warden's liable to get enthusiastic and bring in TV crews and talent scouts after. They'll make a big thing of us. And worse, people like Joey and Jeb are really good. That's going to make some guards feel like they're worse than convicts. Worse than dirt. Can't have that happen to them. They'll take it out on the choir, wreck the choir, so they can re-establish their rightful pecking order.

Miss Julia nods. She's not dumb. She can see the problem. She an' Cory talk for a long time, an' at the end they think they've got a solution. Then she explains it to us cons in the choir. We don't like it. Still, we can see why it's needed. Means more work for us too.

29. Anger Management

Don't know what they do at other facilities. At Dildo correctional, some cons come with special handling instructions. The guards are supposed to know the handling instructions. Part of the guards' duty. An' not a big part seein' there's no more than a handful of special instructions.

Things like George's an epileptic, here's what you do ifn' he has a fit, or Harv's a diabetic, here's what to do ifn' he passes out. I have an instruction attached to my file that says: vegetarian, do NOT give him meat to eat, do NOT make him handle meat in the kitchen. By order of the Warden his'self.

We got a new guard, name of McCreedy. Didn't bother to read his special handlin' instructions. Didn't understand or want to understand why I'm getting special food one lunch time in the canteen. Got nasty about it until Officer Harrison took him aside an' pointed out the special handling instructions, an' the part of by order of the Warden his'self.

So McCreedy backed off, but he was pissed about having to back off. So he does a creative thing for a guard that's pissed. To get over his anger he sends me to an anger management course in the jail. Dildo runs these courses for cons. Supposed to make them better people. The course I'm sent to is run by a civilian named Parker. I've bin on this sort of course before so I know what not to do.

See, the instructor prods at you to make you angry. Then shows you that you've got an anger problem. Then works on you to fix it.

Always seemed a little unfair to me. Like prodding a caged dog with a stick until he snaps at you. Then beat him for snapping at you. Our conversation was about as useful as a milking pail for a bull.

Parker: I hear you get angry at the food in the canteen. Is that right?

Me: No sir.

Parker: Officer McCreedy says you got angry.

Me: No sir. Office McCreedy must be mistaken.

Parker: You find that people around you often get things wrong or lie about you.

Me: No sir. Most times people get things right.

Parker: I notice you don't say anything about people lying.

Me: I think Officer McCreedy was mistaken.

Parker: But you deny you were angry, even though Mr. McCreedy says so.

Me: That's right, sir. Officer McCreedy was mistaken.

Parker: But you refused to eat meat at lunch. Is that right?

Me: That's right sir. I'm a vegetarian. I don't eat meat at any lunch, supper or breakfast.

Parker: Is that a religious conviction?

Me: No sir. It's a medical thing. I have a phobia about it. I'm allergic to meat.

Parker: There's no such thing as an allergy to meat.

Me: (silence).

Parker: You didn't say anything.

Me: Beggin' your pardon, Sir. Didn't hear a question.

Parker: I'm saying there's no such thing as an allergy to meat. How do you respond to that?

Me: I hear your opinion, Sir.

Parker: It's not just an opinion. It's a fact. How do you respond to that?

Me: I hear your opinion that it's a fact.

Parker: But you feel I'm mistaken.

Me: (Silence)

Parker: You didn't say anything.

Me: Was there a question, Sir?

Parker: Damn it. This is not Jeopardy or some quiz show. I'm asking if you think I'm mistaken.

Me: Yes, Sir.

Parker: Like Officer McCreedy?

Me: Yes, Sir.

Parker: So, already we know of two people around you that you believe are full of mistakes about you. Is that right?

Me: Two people, yes, Sir.

Parker: How does that make you feel that the world is full of people who are mistaken about you?

Me: Two people, Sir.

Parker: And does that make you angry?

Me: No, Sir.

Parker: Why not.

Me: No point me getting' worked up about it. It's up to you, Sir, what you think, not me. There's seven billion people in the world. On any day there's prob'ly a billion thinking up some pretty strange things. Ifn' I was to get worked up about it, I'd prob'ly never sleep. I'd lose weight an' die. No point trying to control what others do.

Parker: You'd lose weight an' die if we forced you to eat meat then?

Me: That's what almos' happened when I first came to this facility, Sir.

Parker: What?

Me: The facility didn't like my being a vegetarian for non-religious reasons. Tried to force to eat meat. I didn't eat. After a month there was a fuss about me nearly dying. The regular prison doctor was on vacation. An outside doctor stood in for him. Looked at me, read my files, an' made a fuss, understood why I won't eat meat, called in a congressman, called in the ACLU, threatened to have the State Medical Board disbar the prison doctor an' psychologist, threatened to go to the newspapers. The Warden, didn't want that kind of publicity for the facility. He's issued a special handlin' instruction. I'm to get vegetarian food only.

Parker: I see. Did that make you angry?

Me: No, sir. I was grateful to the outside doctor, an' grateful to the Warden.

Parker: How do you feel about Officer McCreedy?

Me: Don't know much 'bout him, him being new.

Parker: What are you in prison for?

Me: I'm a convicted criminal.

Parker: Was the conviction just?

Me: Yes, Sir.

Parker: What was your crime?

Me: The judge put a publication ban on the court proceedings. To protect the victim's family. I'm not supposed to talk about it.

Parker: Are you avoiding answering?

Me: No, Sir. It's all in my records an' file. You can see the publication ban there too.

Parker: OK. Don't tell me the details. Tell me what you were convicted of.

Me: Manslaughter.

Parker: How come you're in a medium to low security prison? We don't get many convicted murderers at Bilbo Correctional.

Me: Manslaughter, Sir. Not murder.

Parker: Still. How come you're in this facility after a manslaughter charge?

Me: Prosecutor an' defence agree there was zero risk of re-offending.

Parker: So I suppose you were angry at your victim?

Me: Silence.

Parker: That was a question. Were you angry at your victim?

Me: No, Sir.

Parker: It was done in cold blood?

Me: Cold blood. Yes, Sir.

Parker: So why weren't you convicted of murder?

Me: I'm not supposed to talk about it. The judge has ...

Parker. A publication ban. I heard you the first time.

Parker: Do you believe in suppressing your anger?

Me: No, sir.

Parker: Why not?

Me: I'm not angry, Sir.

Parker: I have a piñata hanging here. If I gave you a stick would you like to beat on it?

Me: Are there candies inside the piñata?

Parker: No. It's empty. Would you like to beat on it? See how many blows it takes you to open it up. The record is four blows.

Me: Not much point, Sir.

Parker: Are you on the farm chain gang?

Me: Sometimes.

Parker: I hear the chain gang often have to wait in a hot bus on the farm before they can be let out.

Me: That's right, Sir. We have to wait until the truck with the armed guards arrives.

Parker: Do you get angry having to wait in a hot bus?

Me: No, Sir.

Parker: Got to feel angry, right? You're boiling just because the armed guards are slow. Even the driver and unarmed guard won't wait with you in the hot bus. They can get out and cool down outside. Got to make you angry, right?

Me: No, Sir.

Parker: Why not?

Me: Way I see it, Sir, I got a choice between being hot, or being hot an' angry. I figger it's better to be just hot.

Parker: Do you get on with the other inmates.

Me: Yes, Sir.

Parker: Ever been in a fight with one of them.

Me: I had a shoving match one time with a guy called Wil Sorrel. Guard broke it up real quick.

Parker: You didn't like him?

Me: Didn't hold it against him. It's a guard's job to break up fights.

Parker: Not the guard. Damn it. I meant Sorrel. You didn't like him?

Me: I felt sorry for him.

Parker: Why?

Me: Sorrel heard voices. Voices said I was the knight with the red shield an' he had to challenge me to a joust. Seems that's an old style word for a fight with swords, shields, lances an' the like.

Parker: So how did you feel when he pushed you?

Me: Surprised. Didn't have a shield, an' ifn' I did I wouldn't paint it red anyhow.

Parker kept digging, dug over the same field half a dozen times without turning up any gold. Like I said, Parker's game is prod the dog with a stick 'til it bites. Some cons think their game is to make Parker angry before they get angry. Tell you what, that's a losing game. I don't want Parker angry. I want him tired of the game, take his stick with him an' go home.

Which is what happened after a session or two. Think he was angry as well. Wrote a lot of nasty things in my file. Said anger management techniques would not help until I owned up to my deeply suppressed rage. Said I had an unco-operative nature an' problems with authority figures hiding behind my passive-aggressive stubbornness.

Don't know what much of that means. Strikes me Parker is one frustrated, angry man. Might help him ifn' he beats on that piñata some days. Maybe he does.

30. Low Dog Again

When Low Dog comes out of solitary, after the thing with the math class an' inequality, he also gets told to see Parker.

I got riled about that. Ifn' ever there was a guy with a problem with authority that's Low Dog. Parker doesn't see it though. Low Dog jokes an' laughs with Parker the whole session. I hear Parker writes in LD's file – very balanced personality – no treatment needed.

31. Wil Sorrel an' Cory

Things with Sorrel might have stayed ugly. Cory though, goes an' tells Sorrel I'm Sir Lancelot, the most honourable knight of all. Says my red shield is just a way for me to stay in-cog-nito. Keeps the autograph hunters and press photographers away. Says you can't hunt for the Holy Grail ifn' your picture's in People Magazine. Can't hunt for the Grail ifn' National Enquirer is giving everyone the lowdown on your sex life. Says how could Lancelot hunt for the Holy Grail if the tabloids are saying he's got a thing on the side with Arthur's wife? Cory tells Sorrel the whole thing between me and Guinevere is cooked up by the tabloids, and the thing between me and Guinevere never happened.

After that Sorrel swears allegiance to me an' asks me to knight him. He an' me are OK again. I offered Cory some tobacco for that. Which he didn't take. Never did find out what a holy grail is.

I know a bit about some of Cory's early scams. When he was a young guy. One of his first was the Main Street Diner scam. More a prank then a scam. Still, the bug for scamming bit him round about then. Don't know that Cory has ever been able to see the difference between a prank an' a scam from that day forward.

Anyhows, seems in the town where he grew up in there was a diner, called the Main Street Diner. Main Street Diner was on the outside of the town, north of the rail tracks. Was a bit of a meeting place for the townies around there an' the farming families. The county road crews would have their coffees there in the mornin' before heading out. The sheriff an' his folk would have donuts there at about ten. Rail maintenance crew would stop by for lunch. Ifn' it was too wet to work the fields the farmers would be there most of the morning shooting the breeze.

Anyways, one Thursday night a month they have this local talent night. Cory says talent nights is long on sentiment and short on talent. Girls read "Poem to my Ma", guys play guitar and sing love songs to their girls. Backed up by the on-stage house band. Teenagers with a garage country an' western band do a couple of numbers. An old guy shows off a new juggling trick he's practicing. Twelve-year old farm boys show their new magic shtick, learned from The Boys Book of 101 Magic Tricks. Stuff like that. The diner offers small prizes, draws a big crowd, 'cause every performer has a big family, an' people buy wings, burgers, steak dinners, beer.

So Cory an' his friend Eric approach the manager of the Main Street Diner. Cory points to Eric an' says – this is Mr. Jacques DuBeau. He's France's most famous Saxophone player. Star of French radio and TV. Mr. DuBeau is considering a tour of the USA – mainly New York, LA, San Fran, maybe New Orleans. Before launching the tour he'd like to test audience reaction somewhere in the real US heartland. Wants to do it without any big publicity, without TV crews or press. Just a quiet test to get to know the pulse beat of real people outside of those phoney big cities. Mr. DuBeau speaks no English. Cory is his manager and will translate for Mr DuBeau.

Cory says they've heard about Thursday talent nights at the diner an' it's perfect for what they've been searching for. They want Mr. DuBeau to do a number or two for the crowd next talent night.

The manager is beyond excited. Of course they can do an opening number for the talent night. It's an honour.

It's a pri-ve-lege, an' such like words.

They swear him to secrecy. No advance publicity. Cory's instincts for confidence trickery are already good – swear the mark to secrecy – just like he got non-disclosure agreements from the bank note companies years later. Thursday he an' Eric show up with a saxophone. The manager is on the lookout for them an' takes them into a private dining room for a swank surf-an'-turf dinner with him an' a pretty good bottle of California wine. On the house, compliments of the manager.

As part of the prank, Eric can't talk – 'cause he's not supposed to understand English. Cory has to make conversation with the manager for both of them. Occasionally Cory gabbles at Eric in what is supposed to be French, supposedly translating what the manager is saying. Cory's describing Eric's saxophone history to the manager. How Mr. DuBeau was an orphan without a future, a pickpocket and a small-time teenage crook headed for a bad future, until his musical talent was discovered by accident by French film star Yves Montand, who then became mentor to this new talent.

How Cory makes these things up out of nowhere an' nothin', just on the drop of a hat is a mystery. Unprepared. I've seen Cory do it a dozen times. It's like scratching ground over a Texas oil well an' seeing the black gold gush out from barren soil.

The manager is hypnotized. He's in the presence of one of the world's truly remarkable stars. Mr. DuBeau.

Course, the only part of this that's true is that Eric is a small-time crook. When he lived in Chicago, as a teen, his racket was he had copies of the keys to all the self-serve luggage lockers at Union Station. Amazing all the crooked things people think of. Don't think those self-service luggage lockers exist anymore, but when Eric was a teenager there they had 'em. Ifn' you arrive in Chicago on the morning train, say, an' you're leaving in the afternoon, say, you might want to see the sights. But you don't want to carry your luggage all over town. For seventy-five cents pushed into a coin slot you get the key to one of a hundred luggage lockers. You put your bags in there, lock it up, take the key in your pocket an' see the sights of the city. When you get back you unlock your locker, get your luggage, leave the key in the locker an' board your train. All's well. Unless Eric found something good in your luggage, in which case you board your train with less than you came with.

The beauty of the scam for Eric, is that even ifn' people notice something missing before their train leaves, most don't report it. Don't want to be delayed an' miss their train.

The other part that is kinda' true is that Eric plays sax. Not bad, not great, but good enough for a scam, an' better than most of what gets played at the Main Street Diner.

Anyhows, the manager is hypnotized. Cory 'an Eric get their free meal. The manager takes 'em to the stage. The talent show is in full swing. Manager gets on stage an' tells the audience he has a surprise for them. All the way from Paris, France. Mr. Jacques DuBeau. The world's most famous sax player. The crowd gets real quiet. Eric an' Cory step on stage. Cory looks at the on-stage house band.

He points at the guitarist an' base guitarist an' says just four words – you an' you, off.

Then he points to the pianist an' says – ifn' you play with Mr. DuBeau you play quietly.

To the drummer he says – you got brushes?

The drummer nods.

Cory says – use brushes only, no sticks. The drummer nods.

Cory has a quick conference with them.

Says – Mr. DuBeau's going to play "Take Five".

Can they follow along? They're not sure, they'll try.

Eric plays "Take Five". Folks at the Main Street Diner are into either church music, rock or country. Have prob'ly never heard jazz before. It's new, it's unusual, the beat grips them. Eric keeps it short enough to give them a taste, an' not long enough for them to judge his playing too closely. They stand up an' stomp an' holler when Eric finishes. He bows deeply. The manager has organized a little girl to come up with roses for Eric an' Cory. They bow again. Manager asks for more tunes but they cannot. They're bound by the terms of Mr. DuBeau's recording contract. Manager, shakes hands on stage, thanks them on stage, gives them each another bottle of not bad California wine an' they leave.

Eric's sweating, feels like he's going to throw up. The stress of not speaking an' performing an' playing a role. Cory's used to scams an' pranks, but for Eric this is new. This is not like lockers at Union Station. Eric needs a drink. Eric needs to speak again. In English. Eric needs to stop pretending he's French. They head a mile up the road to The Leprechaun Bar.

They're sitting there with their faces in their first beer when this old farmer walks in. He'd been at the Main Street Diner too. Bad luck he had to walk into the Leprechaun as well. Comes up to their table.

Says – Mr. Jacques DuBeau – that was magnificent – never heard anything like it before – all the way from Paris – wait 'til I tell the wife. Farmer holds out his hand to shake.

For Eric it's the last straw, he can't keep up his side of the scam, it's supposed to be over now. Says – get your hand away from my goddamn beer, an' fuck off back where you belong.

32. Eric

One time I asked Cory what Eric is doing now. Cory says they lost touch years ago. Last he heard Eric was in the HVAC spare parts scam.

Any time I think I've figgered out all the ways people can be crooked, I hear of a new way. Endless ways in the world to be crooked.

I ask Cory – what's that?

He explains it. Cory's always surprised at my innocence. Says it's like explaining candy to a child. Says HVAC is the heating, ventilation and air-conditioning industry. Eric sets himself up as a parts supplier. Got a legitimate business. That's what's sweet about the HVAC scam. Half your business is legit an' no-one can touch you for the other half.

Works like this. Say a home owner has a hot water heater. Gives the house its hot water. Heated by natural gas. It's four years old an' the electronic temperature an' gas control valve breaks. Complicated, expensive. Homeowner calls Eric for a replacement part. Homeowner has forgotten there's a six year warranty on his heater. Six years is typical of the industry. Long enough for homeowners to forget it's still under warranty. Eric tells him the part is $500. Homeowner pays. Now Eric calls the manufacturer, gives 'em the serial number of the heater an' the part number.

They look at the serial number an' say – that one's under warranty still for two more years. We can tell from the serial number. Got the manufacture date embedded in the serial number. We'll send you a replacement, free. No charge.

Now Eric gets the free part an' sends it on to the homeowner. The scam is Eric doesn't tell the homeowner it's under warranty. Doesn't reduce the price. Charges him full price.

An ifn' the one homeowner in a million ever comes back after to Eric, an' says – I just figured out that was still under warranty?

No problem. Eric blames the manufacturer.

Says – don't know why they didn't tell me. How am I supposed to know? You didn't tell me it was under warranty. Why you only telling me now?

'Course he does sell lots of parts that really aren't under warranty. Pays his taxes to the IRS regular. Who's going to know that he regularly scams half his customers?

Ifn' you get Cory talking, you hear about more scams than you ever think are possible.

'Nother time Cory tells me about the India baby scam. Cory likes that one because it's clever, an', he says, no one gets hurt.

Seems many folk in India, when they plan on having a baby, want to choose ahead of time ifn' it will be boy or girl. Maybe millions wanting to have the power to choose ahead of time whether to have a boy or girl baby. So this scammer sets up a mail-order business. Fills pill bottles with harmless sugar pills. Half the bottles have only blue pills, half the bottles have only pink pills. Ifn' a couple want their baby to be boy they order a bottle of the blue pills. Ifn' the couple want a girl, they order the pink pills. The pills come with instructions, one a day with water and some deep breathing exercise. The future Mom takes one a day until the bottle is empty. Does her deep breathing. The scammer offers a money-back guarantee.

Makes a big deal in his marketing about that - We're so sure of this product, that we will give you a full money-back guarantee. Cast-iron guarantee.

Impressive. So where's the scam?

Not being the brightest light, I don't see the scam. How's the scammer going to make money on this?

Cory has to explain it.

Says – look Pango. 'Magine you're a mother to be. You've just taken one-a-day of my pink pills. Done your deep breathing. So you're expecting it to be a girl. Now, tell me what are the chances you really will have a girl?

I finally get it.

Right – says Cory – 50% of the Moms are totally happy. 50% are never going to ask for money back. They believe these pills are the best thing since Kali brought four hands to the Kama Sutra. They tell their friends. These pills are great. They're happy to have paid 400 Rupees for this stuff. It's a modern miracle.

An' no-one gets hurt in this scam. If you're a disappointed Mom, write an' the scammer will repay you.

Disappointed Moms can't damage the reputation of the pills. The gushing happy Moms tell their girlfriends – but you must ALWAYS do the deep breathing exercises with the pills. That's why it didn't work for Reena. You know how Reena is. Reena's always in a rush and forgetting things. You can't rush those exercises. The exercises are very important. I was SOOO careful to do them right. Every day. You cannot skip a day. Reena, now, she's always forgetting things like that.

Cory likes that scam. Still, it's not his kind of scam. Cory gets his kicks out of complicated scams. Scams that start like a chess game. Chess game starts real innocent, you move a little pawn. Who notices a pawn? It's the lowest piece on the board. But slowly, slowly you lever all those little pawn movements until you own the whole damn board.

33. Fingers

Parker, the anger management guy, is full of crap. A wannabe expert. Ifn' Parker had done his homework, he'd have read my files. Would have asked me some better questions too. Like – why did you do time in solitary?

Would have found some real anger ifn' he'd dug there. Could even have told him about the Jain and the Greek.

I spent a year aboard a Danish container ship. Liked the ship. Liked the crew even more. The chief engineer was a Bengali. Name of Anand. Followed a religion called Jainism. An old religion, started long before the Hindus. His buddy was the radio officer, Stavros, a Greek. Didn't believe in any religion but thought the old Greek stories had it right. The two of them would argue it out in the wardroom over dinner.

Stavros used to say – listen Anand, it's no good talking about karma and doing good. If the gods have marked you for tragedy, then the brown stuffs going to drop on you, no matter how much good you do or where you go. That's shit from the heavens. The gods send it to you an' you can't duck. That's life.

Anand now, he'd get riled. Which was against his religion. Which would make him even more riled. At Stavros. For getting him riled.

He'd say – Stavros, you're my friend. But now you're being stupid. We are all souls looking for rebirth into better bodies. You have been very bad in a past life. That is why you are now in the body of an idiot that makes his friends mad at him. If you want a better body in your next life, you must practice good deeds in this life. And you must stop talking crap to your friends. Also, you are holding onto the dessert bowl, even though I have asked you twice already to pass it to this side of the table. In your next life you will surely be a cockroach or a dung beetle.

They'd use me as a referee for their endless argument. They'd say – Pango, tell us, which one of us has it right?

Didn't think either of them had it right at the time. After I was convicted, I thought Anand was right. After I was in solitary I thought Stavros had it right.

See, when I first came to Dildo I did work details in the gravel pit. You sit in the dirt and chip at big slabs of stone making little chips of gravel. It's dusty as all getout. An' rain or shine you're outside. When the sun's out you bake. When it rains you sit in a mud bowl. Come back at the end of day covered in either dust or mud. Usually both. Gets into your skin after a while. Turns you grey. Like some movie Frankenstein. Takes years to come out again. Don't know what it does to your insides. Like to your lungs.

Not a real efficient way to make gravel ifn' you're running a business in the real world. But in Dildo our labour is free of charge. An' the Warden's business is keeping us cons busy. Any money he makes from selling gravel is cherry on the icing.

The only good thing about the gravel pit is it's inside the Dildo compound. Inside the barbed wire fences. So you don't get your ankle chained to the next guy. Gives you a bit of movement. 'Specially at cigarette break or lunch time. You can move around. Try to find a more comfortable patch of mud, or a flat stone, to park your rear on.

During lunch I'd sit off to one side of the pit. There was a pile of old wood scaffolding. Hadn't been used in years. It was a spot to lean my back against when us cons had lunch. Was off to the side. Away from the other cons. After a month I noticed a stray Momma cat had nested in the timber pile. She was patchy grey and black. Scrawny as all hell, and very pregnant. Poor little thing. Don't know why she snuck into a prison to find her nest.

I didn't say anything to the other cons. There were some mean types working the stone hammers. Might have taken out their tempers on the poor cat. An' the guards weren't any better.

I can't touch meat, but I got up the gumption to bring her a bit of fish whenever I could. I'd sneak it out in a plastic bag tucked under my shirt. Had a buddy used to work in the mess who'd get me a bit most days.

Us cons on the stonepile would sit an' eat our lunch. When no one was looking my way, I'd stick a bit of fish into the wood pile. Reach in as far as I could and leave it there for her. A week later I noticed Mama Cat had two little orange kittens sucking at her scrawny dugs. Two little still-blind orange things. Felt real bad for them all. Brought more fish than before. Brought some every day. First it was for Momma Cat. When the kittens were old enough to eat fish it was for them too. Paid my buddy in the mess for the extra fish. Tried to do good in a little way. Tried to make up for all the bad in the world. Like Anand used to tell us to do. Felt maybe Anand had the right of his argument with Stavros.

So one lunch time I'm sitting there again. My back to the woodpile. The kittens have gotten a bit used to me. They won't come out from the woodpile but they're near the edge. An' they're pawing my back to see ifn' I got any more fish for them. They don't mewl. Mama Cat has trained 'em. Mewling is dangerous. Brings predators. But I can feel the little pats on my back.

This con called Fingers comes an' sits next to me.

Some prisons have banned cons from having cigarettes an' tobacco for health reasons. Kinda stupid cause it just makes for a huge black market. Anywhows, at Dildo Correctional the Warden doesn't go down that route. Cons are allowed to smoke outdoors during breaks. Cigarettes an' tobacco are allowed.

Fingers isn't eating. He's smoking a roll your own. An' by the aroma he's mixed hisself a 50/50 mix of tobacco an' weed. That's why he's over where I am at the woodpile. Aways from the others so the smell of the weed is blown away. Must have been strong stuff, or maybe more than just weed. 'Cause he was real mellow. So when the bullhorn an' the tin voice shout to say 1pm time for roll call, he just sits there.

I'm not keen to get up 'til he gets up first. Don't want him left behind seeing the kittens.

He won't move.

Then Zabriski an' his damn dog come to chivvy us. Shouts at us to get in line with the others. Now I'm really stuck. I can't move away from the woodpile with Zabriski's dog standing there. I can't march off down to the others and leave Zabriski an' the dog standing behind me. That fuckin' dog will shake the kittens apart like he's opening Parker's stupid piñata.

I'm not the world's swiftest thinker. Still it comes to me. If I act slow enough, Zabriski is going to pull me down to the others – an' pull his damn dog along with him. He'll be pulling me from the front, not standing behind me at the woodpile.

So, I reach over to Fingers. Grab his roll-your-own an'

take a deep pull. Puff the smoke at Zabriski. Say to him an' his hound dog – Woof woof.

Make it a real loud an' scary bark. Hope the kittens get the message. An' crawl back deep into the wood pile.

The dog is pissed at me. Starts to snarl an' show his teeth. Zabriski's plenty pissed too. I'm walking on the edge of a cliff here. An' the view down aint pretty.

I think of Anand an' his encouragement to do good. His encouragement to get rid of evil karma.

So I say to Zabriski, make my voice real slow an' spaced out – Hello Big Zee, my friendly officer. I don't think I can stand up. My knees are acting funny.

An' I do a bit of giggling just to show him how funny my knees are.

Fingers helps the act too. Doesn't mean to. Just can't help it, the state he's in. Says to me – don't be a hog. My turn to have a pull on that.

Reaches out, has a puff, butts out the joint an' then swallows what's left of it. Looks at my knees an' starts giggling too. Slaps his thighs an' starts laughing louder.

Says – Pango's knees are funny.

Zabriski does what I'd hoped for. Wraps the dogs leash around his wrist. Grabs Fingers an me by the shirt. One hand to each of us. Hauls us up an' marches us down to the stonepit. Away from the woodpile. Dragging the dog after him.

Would have been a happy ending. No matter what charges Zabriski brings against me. 'Cept the dog has smelled something in the woodpile. Is straining to get back there.

Zabriski notices. Looks at us an' says – you potheads got a stash in there?

We shake our heads.

He says – we'll sort that out afterwards. First we're sorting you out.

Fingers an' I get all sort of charges thrown at us. Smuggling, contraband, drug possession, drug use, malingering, disregarding orders, dummy insolence. You name it.

The hard evidence is gone, 'cause Fingers swallowed it.

So we don't get criminal charges.

We get solitary confinement.

When I get out of solitary some of the stone gang tell me the dog killed the cats. When Zabriski turned over the woodpile. They said it weren't pretty. No surprise to me. Knew the cats were dead. Knew it the moment the dog sniffed them. Knew I'd killed them. Knew it going into solitary.

I never felt so low. If I'd left the cats alone they'd still be alive. Had tried to do good and it didn't help a damn.

34. Solitary

All this was in my early days in Dildo. Long before Julia an' the choir. Long before Parker did his anger management sessions with me.

In Dildo solitary there's no books, no magazines, no TV. The guards don't speak to you. You don't see them. Food comes in through a slot in the door. There's a small panel in the door that pulls back, just big enough for an eye to watch you. That's the most human contact you have during solitary. An' most cons don't like the eye watching us. Pretty crappy human contact. More like a machine watching you than a person. I've known cons who shout an' scream at the eye like it's a thing on its own, without a person attached. There's this tough glass panel on the inside of the door to protect the eye. I've known cons who beat on the glass when the eye is watching. Gener'lly, the eye just keeps on watching.

Knew of one con at Dildo who smeared his porridge over the glass panel to stop the eye watching him. Leastways I think it was just porridge. Might have been something worse. The SRT came, pepper sprayed him, and kept him on the floor in chains while the glass got cleaned off. Then they released him from the chains, an' he was back where he started. In solitary. With the eye watching.

There's different ways of keeping your crap together in solitary. Some cons do these long 'rithmetic calculations. Things you'd normally want paper, pencil and calculators for. Get real good at it sometimes. Some cons sing, make bad poems, recite them to the walls. Or recite long lists of things. Some cons slowly scratch drawings on the wall with bits of mortar an' stone chips they've worked loose from somewhere else in the wall. Cell I was in had scratchings of men and women with huge private parts. Some cons do exercise, or meditation. The idea in the meditation thing is to get so quiet that you can feel your heart beating inside you. Not just in your chest. Inside every part of you, arms, legs, chest. Some cons get angry. Turn against the outside world. Convince themselves that they can live like kings in a tiny cell. Don't want anything to do with the outside world. Even turn down their option of one hour of exercise per day outside their cell.

Told you I went into solitary feelin' as low as I've ever felt. On account of having led the damn dog to where Momma Cat an' her kittens were hidin' out.

That's a poor attitude to take into solitary. 'Cause you need somethin' good in your head goin' in, just to keep your head screwed on right.

So, I made conversations in my head with people I used to know. Not my kids. Other people. I never wanted to tell my kids about bad days in Dildo. Even in my head. Always tried to sound OK for them. An' I couldn't talk to Maia, my wife, in my head while I was in prison. She was such a happy person. Couldn't bear to make her unhappy with prison talk – even in a 'magined conversation. Couldn't even think of her after I was in prison. Wouldn't have been right.

But Anand and Stavros were perfect for talking to in solitary. To keep my head level.

Anand came into my head an' said "Pango, my friend, I'm sorry to tell you, for a Jain, what you have done is very bad. Jains and Buddhists are different. If I was a Buddhist I'd say your intentions with the cats were good, and that's all that matters. But we Jains, we say differently. We say it's not just your intentions that matter. It's the outcome. And the result was very bad, my friend. I don't know what to tell you. Of course, if you didn't feed the cats and they died, it would be just as bad."

Stavros said "Anand, stop filling Pango's head with nonsense. The world is simple. If the gods want to take a dump on him they will. They'll simply hang their butts off the side of Mt. Olympus and let fly. Nothing Pango does will change that. The best he can do is hold his nose and keep the soap and water handy. They eat a lot of fruit on Mt. Olympus. Feed each other figs, grapes, pips and all. High fibre. We Greeks have known that for thousands of years. We figured it out about the time we invented democracy, the city state, the right angle, logic and how to sink ships with parabolic mirrors."

Anand got riled of course.

Said "Stavros, if you knew how to read Sanskrit you'd know we Jains were inventing trigonometry a thousand years before your Archimedes. We were inventing trigonometry, negative numbers and the number zero when your forefathers were still counting on their fingers. An' even with their fingers they could only count 'til five. Ha. Not ten, five. Because they used the right hand index finger to tap on the left hand fingers they were counting on. On their left hand. Yes, my friend. Ridiculous. Barbaric. Barbarous. Like this. One, two, three, four, five, many. Do you hear that, Pango? After five comes 'many'. That's how they counted. Now I try to be fair. We Jains are always fair. Open minded. I admit, of course, the advanced Greeks could count to fifteen. But only in summer if they were barefoot and sitting down. Then they could tap on their toes too with the right hand index finger. That's why the important calculations were only done in summer. Things took a long time to figure out for the ancient Greeks. Having to wait until next summer to calculate everything. No wonder the Trojan War took ten years." He paused and huffed. "Now see what you have done, Stavros. You've made me angry again. That is bad karma for my soul. And it is your fault. Your evil karma will surely turn you into a cockroach on the next turn of the wheel, if I don't first beat you into a dung beetle look-alike in this life."

Stavros looked at him and said "Anand, part of what you say I fully believe. That the Jains discovered the number zero – the big nothing, that I believe. I even tell it to my friends. When I talk about you to my other friends I say, 'my friend, Anand, is a Jain. He comes from a very ancient tribe. Can you imagine what they discovered? Long before us Greeks?' My friends say 'What?' I say 'Nothing'. Then I say to them 'You know what's worse? When we have a friendly discussion in the wardroom after supper, he gets so angry he won't pass me the Johnny Walker whisky bottle. Even though I've asked him twice, and my glass is empty. Why is he holding onto that bottle? Like a mother cuddling a newborn.'" Stavros, looked at me and shook his head, "Pango, you know, Anand shouldn't even be drinking alcohol. For a good Jain alcohol is a bad thing, it is self-harm, it harms the actions and the mind. But there he sits cuddling the bottle to his bosom like some street corner drunk, refusing to pour me one tiny dram. Pango, tell us – is that a right action?"

"Ha", says Anand to Stavros, "You dare talk to me about drunkenness. How long did your great Odysseus take to sail home from Troy to Ithaca? Answer me that. Ten years. Again. Another ten years after the Trojan War. I don't know why I bother debating with you, Stavros.

You probably think the Trojan War was about a condom shortage in your neighbourhood pharmacy on Valentine's Day. But ten years! Now, Stavros, we've sailed the Med together you and I. How long does it take from Troy to Ithaca, from modern day Canakkale, Turkey to Ithaca Greece? That's barely 500 nautical miles. Am I right, Pango? If you sail only by day, and average only 4 knots, how long does that take? Let me do the arithmetic for you, my ancient Greek friend. So that you don't have to take off your shoes and count on those ugly toes. That's 40 nautical miles per day. Very easily done. Odysseus should have been home in 14 days. Why did it take him 10 years? Answer me that my Greek friend. I'll tell you what it was: He was seasick. He hated getting aboard any kind of ship. Especially when the Meltemi was blowing up a chop on the water. So he sat in taverns and drank away his fare. Became a class A drunkard. It took him ten drunken years to get the courage to go home across a piffling 500 nautical miles. And then my friend, he had to explain it to his wife, Penelope. He said to her 'Penny my dear, I came as shoon as I could, but there were monshters, witchesh, giantsh, cyclopsh.' Ha. And she pretended to believe him. Better to let it go then explain why she was caught in the middle of a drunken orgy with dozens of so-called 'suitors' that she liked to swing with. She had big appetites, that woman. And her husband was missing, believed dead, for ten years. Of course she wasn't celibate. Someday I, Anand, will write the true history of the Odyssey, based on hard geographic facts about the miserable 500 mile journey that took him 10 years. And what did Odysseus get drunk on in those island taverns, my fine Greek friend? On retsina. The foulest drink that ever a thirsty sailor had to pay good money for. That's what you like to drink, Stavros, and now you ask me to waste good whisky on you. Never! Get your hands off my whisky bottle."

"Come, Anand", Stavros said. "After years of sailing with you, I know about Jains. What does your religion say about non-possessiveness? Jains say possessiveness is a sin. You have taught me the word in your language: aparigrahaIt. That, Pango, is the Jain word for what Anand must strive for. It means non-possessiveness. I say it each night when I gargle before bed. Sometimes I even say it backwards. It is a sin for a good Jain to become attached to possessions like a Johnny Walker whisky bottle. Anand, pour our friend Pango a dram, and then out of great generosity of spirit pour me and you a dram too. Then I will propose you a toast, such as only Stavros can propose. Good. Good, our glasses our full. There Anand, I knew you had generosity in you. Thank you. Efcharistó."

Stavros bowed to us both without spilling a drop from his full glass. He went on "Now you are ready to hear my interesting toast. I start again with the gods taking a dump on Pango's head. A Christian would look up at the heavens and say 'Lord Zeus, for what we are about to receive, may we be truly thankful.' A Muslim would say 'Inshallah'. It is as God and Allah wills it. A Buddhist would say if Pango's intentions are good then it doesn't matter that Zeus craps on him. Ha! You Jains tell poor Pango that if the outcome of what Lord Zeus is about to let fly onto Pango's head is bad, then it's Pango's fault. Listen now to what I, Stavros, would say. Here is my toast. Stand up, you two heathens. Raise your glasses with me. Clink. Like so. Now we say together, I will speak slowly and you repeat after me:

Lord Zeus

And all fellow gods

And immortals

Who dwell on Olympus
Stavros, Anand and Pango
Wish you
Ten thousand years
Of total constipation.

And when the ten thousand years are over
Lord Zeus
And all fellow gods
And immortals
Who dwell on Olympus
Stavros, Anand and Pango
Ask respectfully
Please dump on someone else.

Now I don't have any 'magination. Most of those
conversations with Anand and Stavros I'd heard before.
In real life. On the Danish container ship. They talked like
that most evenings. Was kind of fun to replay them in my
head. Splice bits an' pieces together in new ways. Helped
me keep my head straight sitting there in solitary. Made
me laugh out loud some days. Officer Harrison heard me
laughing in solitary one time an' got a bit worried 'bout
my health. Heard 'bout that afterwards. At the time, all I
saw was an eye in the door panel watching me while I
laughed.

'Course, it wasn't all beer cans an' turkey shoots in
solitary. I had my down days too. Plenty of them.

Another thing 'bout solitary. I was always hungry.
More than usual. See what happens is solitary at Dildo is
a reduced calorie diet. 'Cause you're not working the
gravel pit or Hoovers. So you're hungry to start with.

Then, I have this thing. I need to keep reserves of food nearby. Just in case. So I used to put bits of my meal on the window sill of my cell. Bits of sandwich, a piece of apple. Stuff like that. I'd build up a reserve. An' until I'd built the reserve, I'd have to eat less. Then on about day three, this little red bird with a black face took to flying onto the window sill and pecking at my food reserves. Heard later it's called a Cardinal. The bird I mean. Real cute little guy. So then I had to build up a new reserve in a corner of the cell. For myself. An' put by a bit of food each day for the little bird.

He an' I would have regular conversations there. Made solitary less solitary. I'd recite lists for him, lists of sailor stuff. Test my memory with the little bird. Some days I'd recite lists in German or French or Japanese. Think he liked it. We got so that he'd sit on my fingers an' take bread crumbs off my hand. Strange feeling those tiny little feet gripping my fingers.

He also dropped a little red feather on my window sill. Didn't notice it when it happened. The next time I put food out I found it. What with time being plentiful in solitary, I spent hours staring at it. Felt the softness and wondered how it would be to fly out of there with wings. It was quite something. Nothing else in solitary with me as bright or as soft as that. Just hard grey concrete. I kept the feather for years after, 'til it finally fell apart.

By day six the little bird started bringing his wife along for a piece of my sandwich. She was less colourful than he was. Liked my sandwiches though an' sang real nice. So then I'd put out extra for her. Used to sing songs for her. What with me feedin' the two of them an' keepin' reserves for myself, I was always hungry.

35. Full Moon and Knock-Knock

The window in my cell in solitary had no glass. Like I said, the guards don't want cons loading up with sharp pieces of broken glass. So the window was just an empty opening in the concrete with bars on. There was no air conditioning in the cells. The window was it. Let some air in on hot days. An' it let the birds fly in and share my food. Kept me company. It also let me see the time of day – sunrise, sunset, moonrise an' such. I liked that. I could see the sky, nothing else. Looked at clouds, saw if there was wind up high, watched the colours of the sky change at morning and night. One time I saw a leaf being blown around. It did spirals up an' down. Stayed there for the longest time. Just where I could see it looking up through the narrow window from my cell. Like the leaf was staying right outside my window on purpose. Giving a poor con a special show. Just for me. It was real special. Better than any air show I've ever seen with jets an' barnstormers an' parachute jumpers. To make me feel better. Bucked me up no end.

When I first went into solitary there was just me and Fingers. He was a few cells down from me. After a few days inside I saw it was full moon. Saw the moon come up in a big white full circle. Reached its high point around midnight, like full moons do.

There's a belief in prisons that full moons bring on trouble. More violence, more suicides, more sickness, more injuries, more cons going crazy. Never believed it myself. Think it's an old wives' tale. You get those troubles any day of the week in prisons. Still, while I was in solitary something happened 'round full moon time in the rest of the prison. The next day I heard doors in solitary near me opening and three cons being put in. Lots of shouting and cursing and doors slamming shut. Couldn't tell who the cons were or what ruckus they'd gotten up to. But for sure it was full moon an' there they were.

No way of talking to them. A whisper wouldn't reach them. An' shouts carry but you can never hear what the words are saying. Just a noise. The echoes and the cell doors cover up the words. In any case, you start shouting an' soon the SRT is pepper spraying you in your cell or beating on you with clubs. Not a good idea.

Same problem if you knock or bang on the cell wall. The walls are thick concrete. The guy next door ain't going to hear it.

There was one way to find out what was going on. It's called the knock-knock code and it's been around prisons forever. Strange thing is not every con knows how to work it. I first heard about it from a Guatemalan con called Jaime. Before I went into solitary. He was a political prisoner in Nicaragua. Said the politico prisoners there used the knock-knock code. Explained to me how it goes. It's a bit complicated at first. So at Dildo some cons have never heard of it. An' if they have, only half can use it, 'cause you have to be able to read an' write an figger it out. 'An half the cons in solitary are too angry at the world to want talk to anyone. So I figgered there was maybe one in ten chance that one of the newcomer cons in solitary would answer. Still, I had the time to try.

Every cell in solitary has its own toilet an' wash basin. 'Cause solitary prisoners don't get to leave the cell for washing or using the toilet. Means the cells are connected. By the plumbing pipes. So if you tap on, say the cold water pipe coming to your washbasin, the guy in the next cell might hear your tapping. Waited 'til night time when it's quiet so that the other cons might hear the code. Then started tapping 'hello', over and over.

Like I say, it's a bit complicated. An' slow. But I had time. It's not Morse code. Us cons don't know Morse. An' anyway for Morse you need two kinds of sound. The water pipe only makes one kind of sound. An' the knock-knock code is simpler than Morse.

What you do, for English anyway, is you shrink the alphabet to just 25 letters. You forget about 'K', you can use 'C' instead. That leaves 25 letters. Put the 25 letters on a five by five grid. Five rows, five columns. The first row is 'A, B, C, D, E' an' so on like this:

	1	2	3	4	5
1	A	B	C	D	E
2	F	G	H	I	J
3	L	M	N	O	P
4	Q	R	S	T	U
5	V	W	X	Y	Z

That way every letter has a row number an' a column number. That's the code for the letter. If I want to tap the code for the letter 'H', I tap two times to show it's a letter in row 2, an' three times to show it's in column 3.

So there I was, night after full moon, in solitary, tapping on my cold water pipe:

2-3, 1-5, 3-1, 3-1, 3-4

Then I'd wait. See if there was any answer. An' hoped it wouldn't be Fingers answering 'cause I was still mad at him. For sitting next to me at lunch.

No answer from anyone.

Then I'd tap again.

2-3, 1-5, 3-1, 3-1, 3-4

And wait again.

Did that for an hour or two. Then got bored and did it for another hour or two to kill time.

2-3, 1-5, 3-1, 3-1, 3-4

Pause.

2-3, 1-5, 3-1, 3-1, 3-4

Pause.

2-3, 1-5, 3-1, 3-1, 3-4

Pause.

2-3, 1-5, 3-1, 3-1, 3-4

Pause.

Over and over.

Never did get an answer.

Anyhows, just to help out future cons I scratched the grid into the concrete wall in my cell over the next few days. Used a loose piece of concrete and scratched it out real neat in a low corner of the cell, where the guards might never see it.

After I got out of solitary I heard that one of the other cons in solitary near me had complained to a guard. Said how was he supposed to sleep in solitary with all the noises in the plumbing? Said that was sleep deprivation, cruel an' unusual punishment, an' he wasn't standing for it, said if it happened again he'd lodge a formal complaint with The Warden. So the next day, instead of giving him his hour of exercise the guards came an' listened to his plumbing for two minutes. Heard nothing of course. 'Cause I only did it one night. Guards weren't too happy with the con. Told the con that was his exercise hour for the day. Told him if he gave 'em any more frivolous complaints they'd charge him an' double his time in solitary.

36. Knock-knock for Geniuses

After solitary I told Jaime I'd tried his knock-knock code. Jaime had a good story about knock-knock.

Seems that in the days of Stalin a Russki, name of Alexei, in a Moscow prison deciphered the code without help. Alexei had been pulled off the street by the KGB. No one else knew that he was in prison. He could die and no would know. 'Cept the KGB. Every day they tortured him. Wanted him to confess to some 'maginary crime. Every night he thought about killing himself. But then every night the guy in the cell next door was tapping some kind of code at him. Alexei listened. Got some curiosity back. Enough to want to live another night and figger her out. Alexei didn't get it at first. Didn't know the guy next door was typing the Russian version of A, B, C, letter by letter all the way down to Z. Using the tap code. Every night he'd end the alphabet with the same question, the Russki way of asking:

5-2, 2-3, 3-4, 4-2, 4-5?

Took three months, but Alexei finally figgered her out from the pattern of taps 1-1, 1-2, 1-3, 1-4 an' so on. Figgered that that it might be an alphabet. Might be in a grid. The grid thing was his big breakthrough. Once he thought about a grid, the lights came on big time. He took matches and made stick letters with the matches. Laid 'em out in a grid on the floor. So he could see the pattern. Waited another night an' figgered out what the question was. Started a conversation with the other guy. Tapping on the pipes every night. Got back the will to survive. 'Cause someone else wanted to know about him. Every night. Wanted to know if he was living or dying.

Was going through the same crap. Ifn' that guy could survive then Alexei figgered he could survive too. An' ifn' that guy died, Alexei figgered he needed to survive to carry the word back to the outside.

Alexei must have been one giant brain. Maybe politico cons are smarter than us low-life cons. Can tell you I'd've never figgered her out by myself. You could type that alphabet at me 'til the last trumpet an' I'd've been like the guy who complained to the guards. Quit that racket. SHUT UPP. I gotta sleep.

37. Julia Again

Julia. Now that's someone who needs anger management. Man, was she mad at me. See, I had to miss two choir practices to attend anger management with Parker. She was fit to spit roofing nails. Shouted at me for a solid 10 minutes in front of all the cons in the choir.

Shouted - I don't care about your damn anger management. What kind of infantile nerd needs outside help to keep his anger under control? Didn't you learn that at kindergarten? Do you see me needing outside help to stay calm? No wonder you help out in the library. Books don't care that you act like a moron. I'm not finished. Be quiet when you interrupt me. I expect you here at choir practice. This is not a deal where you show up when you want to and miss practice when you don't. I couldn't care less what your excuse is. Lying on the beach is not an excuse. Anger management is not an excuse. Dates with movie stars are not an excuse. Execution and the electric chair is not an excuse. Death is not an excuse. You get off that electric chair and you show up for choir.

The other cons were a little afeared of her carrying on like that. None of them dared to smile while she was ranting. Even ifn' some of the stuff she was spouting was pretty funny. For sure they were all glad it was me an' not them.

I got to thinkin' afterwards that maybe it wasn't so much me she was mad at. Maybe it was nerves at trying to pull of the big performances with a bunch like us. An' the politics that she an' Cory were trying to ride herd on. That wasn't easy for sure.

So I kept quiet while she ranted an' said only – Yes,

Mam. No Mam.

The other reason I kept quiet, was that Jeb was hoverin' behind her like some protective father who's discovered that the village preacher has gotten his twelve-year old daughter pregnant. The madder she got, the madder he looks.

With him so big an' her so small an' young, it really did look like protective father an' young daughter. Took them both a while to calm down.

38. Little Mysteries

I'm on duty for a week to empty the kitchen swill bins after supper. Got to wheel them out full. Leave 'em at the back gate where the farmer comes by to load 'em on his truck.

He carts them off to his hog farm. Feeds the contents to his hogs. Stale bread, stale fruit, fruit with mould, scrapings from cons plates, scrapings from the kitchen pots, potato peels, the leafy parts from the tops of carrots, an' such. Brings back empty bins each time.

Whenever I wheel out full bins, there are empty bins waiting for me to hose out an' bring back to the kitchen. I hose out one of the bins an' notice one of the hinges is bust. A metal hinge pin is missing. Don't think much of it at the time. Just makes the job slower. Should've paid attention.

39. The Inside Show

I got to hand it to Cory an' Julia. They handled the politics of the first show just fine. They did four things to make sure the guards didn't look like bums while the choir was on stage.

First they had Zabriski an' Harrison be masters of ceremony. Zabriski took the first half, Harrison the second.

Second, Harrison joined in a couple of the songs. Wasn't half bad either.

Third, Julia had asked the guards beforehand to select some of the songs from a list she provided. Cory an' she stacked the deck, like a magic card trick. You know. The magician asks you to choose one card from three, an' you always end up choosing the card he wants you to choose. So mostly the guards chose songs we already knew we wanted. There were three that came at us out of left field an' we had to learn special. One was Goodnight Irene, the second was a chanty called Santy Anno, then there was another chanty called Sally Brown. Think Harrison chose the two chanties, an' he sang along with both.

Harrison has a small motor boat somewhere on a lake near Dildo an' fancies himself a sailor. Sings chanties about Cape Horn while fishing in the reeds of the local lake. 'Course the lake is flat calm. It's way better to sing about storms than sail 'em.

Actually us cons got to like those two songs. I sometimes still catch myself humming those:

Heave her up and away we'll go,
Away Santy Anno,
Heave her up and away we'll go,
We're bound for Californio.

Have you heard the latest news?
Away Santy Anno,
The Yanks have taken Vera Cruz,
All along the plains of Mexico, so

Heave her up and away we'll go,
Away Santy Anno,
Heave her up and away we'll go,
We're bound for Californio,

Sailing out of Liverpool,
Away Santy Anno,
The winds were up and the holds were full,
We're bound for Californio, so

Heave her up and away we'll go,
Away Santy Anno,
Heave her up and away we'll go,
We're bound for Californio,

We've a mighty fine ship and a mighty fine crew,
Away Santy Anno
And a mighty fine man for a captain too,
We're bound for Californio, so

Heave her up and away we'll go,
Away Santy Anno,
Heave her up and away we'll go,
We're bound for Californio,

Santy Anno has 10,000 men,
Away Santy Anno,
Santy Anno has 10,000 men,
All along the plains of Mexico, so

Heave her up and away we'll go,
Away Santy Anno,
Heave her up and away we'll go,
We're bound for Californio,

When I leave this ship I'll settle down,
Away Santy Anno,
And marry a girl named Sally Brown,
All along the plains of Mexico, so

Heave her up and away we'll go,
Away Santy Anno,
Heave her up and away we'll go,

All along the plains of Mexico, so

Heave her up and away we'll go,
Away Santy Anno,

Heave her up and away we'll go,
We're bound for Californio.

The other one goes like this:

Well we shipped on board a Liverpool liner,
Way hey row and row;
And we rowed all night and rowed 'til the day,
I'm gonna spend my money on Sally Brown.

Miss Sally Brown is a fine young lady,
Way hey row and row;
And we rowed all night and rowed 'til the day,
I'm gonna spend my money on Sally Brown.

Her mother doesn't like the tarry sailor,
Way hey row and row;
And we rowed all night and rowed 'til the day,
I'm gonna spend my money on Sally Brown.

She wants her to marry the one-legged captain,
Way hey row and row;
And we rowed all night and rowed 'til the day,
I'm gonna spend my money on Sally Brown.

And now we're all rowing down to Valaparaiso.
Way hey row and row;
And we rowed all night and rowed 'til the day,

I'm gonna spend my money on Sally Brown.

Well we shipped on board a Liverpool liner,
Way hey row and row;
And we rowed all night and rowed 'til the day,
I'm gonna spend my money on Sally Brown.

Julia wanted us to sing "roll" not "row". The only argument the cons ever won with her. They wanted to sing "row". She gave up on that one. Allowed us to sing "row".

Fourth thing Julia did for the politics was this. The Warden sat in the audience an' never got on stage once. Still, he an' his wife cheered an' clapped like maniacs.

So the guards, got half a notion that this was their show. The cons were quiet at first. I mean the cons in the audience. Guess they started with the same notion. That this was somehow the guards running the show. There was some mutters from them about that. 'Specially with Zabriski, Mr. Charm his'self, opening the show. When we started singing their songs though, they were wild for us too.

Julia did something for the last two numbers that I'd've never thought of. Real clever. She dropped a huge curtain right at the front of the stage. Some kind of thin white cloth like a giant white bed sheet. Between us an' the audience. We stood behind the curtain. Behind us were lights. The lights shone our shadows onto the white curtain.

We sang "Take this Hammer", swinging our arms an' bodies like men hammering spikes into a railway line. Julia had drilled us on how she wanted it done, in time with the singing. Ifn' we'd done that without the curtain, it would have been corny. An' no way were the guards going to put real hammers into our hands for a show. But with the shadow-men on the bed sheet swinging away it looked like a real chain gang with hammers an' all. Made the song real to the audience.

Same bed sheet for the last number. Our Hoover Farm chain gang song. Alberta, Alberta. This time the shadow-chain-gang were swinging shadow-spades an' shadow-picks. The cons in the audience were on their feet singing with us throughout. Cheered themselves hoarse at the end.

Took about 10 minutes before Julia could get a word in to close the show. She thanked the prison guards an' the warden, didn't say too much about the choir an' shut her down.

Maybe not thanking the choir was another bit of politics.

After the curtain came down though we got hugs from her. Told us we'd done real good. She was proud of us. Some of the cons who hadn't been given a hug in year, much less by a pretty young woman, had tears in their eyes. Even Jeb was smiling. Like a proud father watching an adopted daughter. Don't know how that got into his head, but that's how he looks at her.

40. Intermission

Seems the Warden is really bucked by our choir. Cory's next chess moves goes just as planned. The Warden talks to Julia an' the guards an' the chaplain about doing a show outside the prison walls. Julia's already got a plan. Presents her plan to the Warden. Her college has a large theatre. They'll let us use it. They're keen on it. The music department, the sociology department, the criminology department, the drama department, all kinds of college departments want to get behind this.

The Warden wants press an' local TV to attend an' film our choir.

This is turning into major publicity for The Warden. Shows how progressive he is, shows how he turns hardened criminals into choir boys. Shows how efficient his prison is. He'll find a way to lever that to get extra funding for prison programs. He's quick on his feet, churns out all kinds of new program ideas. Re-in-te-gra-tion. From prison choir to community choir. Might be an idea there. Some of the program money will make its way into his pockets too. Might get a legit raise even. Might run for state or government office someday an' this won't hurt his profile a bit.

The Warden an' Julia settle on details. We'll do the same show at the college that we did at the prison. This time the Warden will be master of ceremonies. Not Zabriski, not Harrison. The local TV channel sends a fellow to sit in on the planning. They talk camera angles for TV, what's going to be on camera before, after an' during. We hear this from Julia.

The Warden talks security an' all. The TV folk want us trooping onto stage looking like reformed cons. They want to push the idea of music having tamed us. So no chains on us on stage, no armed guards on stage. The Warden has to think hard. His ass is on the line ifn' one of us runs for it. He understands that chains an' guards armed with rifles standing on stage behind us won't look right. But he ain't going to gamble.

This is what he comes up with. We get transported the usual way. In chains on the bus. Just like Hoover's Farm. Armed guards follow us in a separate bus. Just like usual. The college will reserve a corner of the big parking lot for our buses. Close to the stage back door. When both buses arrive, a guard will unchain us in the bus an' march us to the stage back door an' into a green room. That's where we wait to go on stage. Armed guards with rifles wait out back. Unarmed guards in the green room, an' in the audience. Two guards with side arms on stage, out of sight of the audience. After the show, back into the bus an' chains back on for the transportation.

Julia tells me there was a lot of talk about whether the Warden had to involve the US Marshals service for transportation. Too much paperwork. He said no. Just our regular prison guards.

The TV guy wants some shots of us practicing inside the prison chapel. Before the big night. Wants some shots of how Julia coaches this or that con on his singing. Show how she's helping them improve. They work through the logistics of bringing a TV crew into the chapel for a Sunday rehearsal.

Warden finally agrees something for next Sunday. Also he wants a shot of Harrison singing with the choir, an' the guards helping with marching the cons in an' out. Maybe some smiling exchanges, between the guards an' the cons as they march. Show the good relations his prison fosters between staff and inmates. Those are his words. Julia tells us. Wants a TV shot of himself droppin' by during the rehearsal to give encouragement. How we perk up an' sing better for knowing he's there.

So the next Sunday the TV crew films us rehearsing. Goes just fine. Someone has the sense to have Sanderson, not Zabriski, march the cons in an' out of rehearsal. Means there's no problem filming a few smiles between the guard an' the cons. Even shows us singing louder after The Warden drops by.

Heard afterwards that Zabriski was pissed at not being filmed for TV an' had a few hard words about it with Sanderson. Those two really don't cotton to each other. Me, I think the TV guys are happy not to film his ugly dial. Don't want the sponsors bailing on the show.

We've got two months to go until the outside show. You'd think that Julia would let us idle. Heck, we know the songs.

Wrong. Letting us idle isn't her nature. She drives us as hard as ever.

We do vocal exercises, we learn new songs, we rehearse our old songs. She tries to see ifn' we can sing still higher or lower than our usual range. Then she's no longer happy with the way we're standing on stage. Got to try shuffling who stands next to whom. See ifn' the sound gets any better. When she's finally happy with that she does another rehearsal. Then she films it an' records us. Uses one of those home video cameras. Makes us watch ourselves. The thing records sound too. Makes us listen to ourselves. Asks us what we think we can do better. Makes everyone say something about themselves an' about someone else. Even Slow Joey. Then we rehearse again.

Get's us listening to some fancy professional choirs on CD an' such. Tells us not to be intimidated. Says they make mistakes. Says that's the sound we can aim for. Let's each one of us say what we think the pros do well or badly. Asks us ifn' we make the same mistakes. Asks us ifn' we can do some of the good things we hear.

Starts us on fancy Yoga breathing exercises every time we rehearse. Fancy names like Cobra, Cat, Extended Puppy, Camel Pose. Some of the cons laugh at that. She reams us all out something fierce. Says she's not a comedian. Here she is doing the best to make us sound as good as we can be. How dare we treat this like a joke after all her hard work. Why aren't we focused on sounding better? Jeb stands behind her an' growls at us. Like he's doing harmony base note while she reams us out. Might be harmony but it ain't pretty.

Another Sunday she brings in a prof from the music department at her college. Has him listen to our rehearsal. He says there's not much to change an' we don't. Says we can have musicians, an orchestra from the college to play with us ifn' we want. Julia an' he kick the idea round some an' finally decide not to mess with the original formula.

Julia has one surprise left for us. Warden has agreed. We're not wearing prison orange on stage. We each get blue jeans an' a blue tee shirt.

Jeans are elastic sided. No belts allowed. Might strangle ourselves or each other. Or loop the belts together an' use 'em as ropes to climb over walls. Guess they trust us not to tie our blue jeans together as a rope to climb over a wall. In our underwear. Still, feels weird in good way to be dressed in something as soft as the tee shirt. An' the jeans. Forgot how stiff new jeans feel. Still, make us feel like for a moment we're back in the real world.

There's a lot of messing about while we get sizes an' fit sorted out. Like kids tryin' on Halloween costumes. Exciting but not quite real.

Hubbard is a con in the choir who could stand to lose a few pounds. Spends too much money in the commissary candies an' soft drink section. He's always clowning. Says to Julia – Mam, does this outfit make me look fat?

She doesn't miss a beat.

Says – No, Hubbard, the jeans don't make you look fat. Your fat makes you look fat. Even Jeb is grinning at that one.

Most of us are fairly easy to fit. A few guys like Hubbard an' Jeb cause most of the size problems.

41. Cottonwoods

Balm in Gilead isn't one of our choir songs. Cory says when we get a regular performance schedule in the outside world we'll do it then. Maybe when we get a recording contract. Patience - he says.

Does get the cons talking again about Balm in Gilead. They start asking Hiero what's a balm?

Turns out Hiero knows. Says it's a medicine. You smear it on wounds, heals the wound, just like the song says. Smear it on aching muscles an' bone too. Used to come from a tree that grew in the Holy Land. Maybe the balsam tree. Says his Grandma used to make something similar from Cottonwood trees. His grandma called that Balm of Gilead too.

All this happens just as the cons are going through a health fad. Prison fads come out of nowhere an' usually disappear after a couple of weeks.

Kind of like those fads at junior school. One week it's yoyos, another week it's trading baseball cards. Who knows why?

Right now at Dildo it's a health fad. Cons buy granola an' energy bars at the commissary instead of chocolate, choose fruit juice an' chocolate milk stead of Coke. Do push-ups in the exercise yard stead of taking metalwork classes. Won't last long. Still, right then everyone wants some Balm of Gilead.

Even Harrison, the guard, wants some. Has a cut on his leg from where the prop on his boat cut him. It ain't healing right. Been weeks now. Maybe that swamp water put some fungus or bacteria in the cut. Maybe carp crap got into the wound. Harrison don't cotton to doctors an' pharmacies. 'Sides which they're expensive. Harrison pulls Hiero aside.

Says – we got some Cottonwoods over on Hoover's farm. What do we do to make this here Balm of Gilead?

Hiero tells him. You need to get branches of Cottonwood that are pushing new buds. If they're sticky an' smell like moth balls, you've got the right kind of Cottonwood tree. Break off the buds. Soak 'em in cooking oil. Heat the whole mess for near on two days. Not boiling, just very hot. Let it cool off for another day. Wrap it all in thin cloth and squeeze out the liquid. Into a clean jar. Leave the buds behind in the cloth. Keep the oil. That's your Balm of Gilead from a Cottonwood. Throw away the cloth an' the buds.

Us cons get excited. Not many new things in a cons life. Next time we're at Hoover's Farm, Harrison has Hiero gathering Cottonwood buds. Turns out it's the right time of year for buds. Looks like they're the right kind of Cottonwood too. Smell like something Hiero calls camphor. Most branches are too high for us to get at so Harrison comes the next time with a rope. Has us tie a stone to the rope. Gets Jeb to toss the stone over a high branch an' drop it over the far side. Now we've got a rope slung over a high branch with two rope ends on the ground. Has a team of us on each side of the rope pulling to break the branches an' pull 'em down to the ground. Works pretty good too as long as you stand clear. Has us bring branches to Hiero. Hiero break buds off. Finishes the day with a fair size pile of buds. Harrison stuff them into five sandwich bags an' five cons hide a bag under their shirts. Guys like Hubbard are over large anyway so no-one will notice.

First time any of us have been asked by a guard to smuggle stuff off the farm into the prison. Hidden. Under our shirts. Harrison must be real worried about his cut leg to do this. Keeps telling us it's not real smuggling. Says Hoover doesn't give a damn about a few cottonwood buds.

Anyhows, the metal shop has an oven for baking paint glazes onto metal. Harrison brings in cooking oil. Arranges over a weekend plus a day to have the oil an' buds heated in that oven. On Tuesday some of the metal shop cons bottle the oil. Everyone who helped gets a little bit. Feels like cooking oil, but smells good.

Harrison puts some on his cut every day for a week. Tells us it's pure gold. His cut starts to heal after two days. It's totally closed after a week. I offer some to Mrs. H. in the library for her 'thritis.

She says – no thank you Pango. I'll stick with what the doctor gives me.

That's a shame. 'Cause Howell has 'thritis in his hands an' I can see the swelling go down.

Hubbard smears some on his ankles. Says they're swollen. After a few days he says he they feel great. I still think his ankles are just as swollen, but whatever.

The biggest success – or maybe not - is Wil Sorrel. Runs round the exercise yard shouting – I can walk again! I can walk again!

Never knew he had trouble walking before. Kind of doubt he did.

Still from then on Hiero's Balm of Gilead has a reputation at Dildo Correctional. Amongst cons an' guards. Stories 'bout Hiero's balm get wilder an' wilder. Some cons take to calling him Saint Hiero, the con with the balm.

42. Black Market

Prisons have a black market. Cons end up doing all kind of stuff. Depends what they're good at. Some carve chess pieces or dominoes from soap bars. Sell 'em for tobacco or credit at the commissary. Guys who work the gravel pit bring back tiny shiny pebbles. Carve numbers on em. One, five, ten, twenty, one hundred. Sell 'em as poker chips for card games.

Others are tattoo artists. Tattoo just about anything on you. Whatever the customer wants. You'd be surprised. A smiley face on the end an' a ruler tattooed down the side of the customer's dick is one of the top ten requests. Got to seeing some cons 'round about then with a tat' that says "The Dildo Choir". Cons were proud of that. Also got to see a few tat's that said "St. Hiero's Balm". Like wearing a cross, or a St. Christopher medallion, or garlic against vampires. The tat' alone is supposed to help against disease. What with all the ruckus about the balm, you can find any number of cons who tell you about the tat' an' the miracle cures the tat' has done.

Me, because I'm studying divinity, or just because I'm studying, cons come to me to ask me with help with reading an' writing. Might be writing to their family, might be how to fill out a prison application form, might be reading a letter from their family or girlfriend. That's a hard one. Cons who need help reading an' writing don't often get letters. An' ifn' they do it's usually bad news. I have to prepare 'em for it before I can read it to them.

Hubbard comes to me with a letter from home, needs help reading it. Had a bad feeling even before I looked at it.

He says – Pango, how much for reading me this letter?

Ifn' the cons are polite, I never charge. Ifn' some guy comes up to me an' says – read this – no please, no thank you, no how much, just ordering me around, then I charge em.

But Hubbard, Hubbard's this cheery big guy, like a Santy Claus in prison orange, never pushy. An' he asks – how much.

I say – Hubbard, we've known each other a while. I'm not gonna charge.

He gives me the letter. I have a quick glance. I think maybe a nurse in a hospital helped write it. Says his wife is in hospital, hit by a car, hit an' run, looks bad, might not make it.

We're in the exercise yard.

I say – Hubbard, why don't we sit over there in the shade. Make it easier for me to read. Can't rightly see in this bright sunlight.

When we're sitting I say – Hubbard, this is bad news. Need you to listen calm like. Can you do that?

He nods.

I read him the letter. He puts a big hand over his face. Reckon he doesn't want me to see his tears.

I say – take your time.

He swallows a couple of times. Needs to work around a lump in his throat. I pat his back. Finally gets his throat back working.

Says to me – guess that St. Hiero's Balm doesn't protect against everything.

I say – no.

He says – Pango, what do I do?

I say - go the chaplain. He's big on family. Show him the letter. Ask him for help filling out the form for compassionate temporary leave. It's the form for 18 US code 3622. Chaplain will know it. Get him to take the form an' this letter to The Warden real fast. Ifn' Warden approves it, you can get out for a few days to be with your wife.

Hubbard comes back to me end of the day. He's looking real bad.

Says – Pango, Warden will approve it if I can pay the travel an' cover the US Marshalls' expenses. They got to accompany me to make sure I don't run. I don't have the money. Pango – what do I do?

We talk a bit. Figger out what it's going to cost. It's not too much. I say I'll lend it to him. He can pay it back whenever. He hesitates. Doesn't know whether to take the money or tell me what's bugging him.

Finally says – Pango, how am I gonna pay you back. When? I got nothin'.

I say – don't matter. I got some put by outside. Might never get to use it. Might die in here. I can lend you the money. Some of the guys, in the choir an' in the dorm, will pitch in too. You'll pay it back ifn' when you can, if not, it's no loss. Go see your wife.

I can see he wants to gives me a hug. Hesitates though. In Dildo that sends the wrong message to all kinds of folk.

So I pat his shoulder an' say – Go see your wife.

He says – God bless you, Pango.

Which would be nice, but it's years too late. The only blessing I got from above was a load of crap dropped on me from Mount Olympus. The stink is still on me. Always will be. Anyhows, he shakes my hand a dozen times instead of the hug. Then he runs off. Not smilin' but still, looks better than when he came.

Choir's gonna have to sing without Hubbard. Thought Julia would have a fit of anger again. When she hears about it she close to near cries. No predicting that one.

43. Showtime

It's the big night. We're in the bus. Heading to Julia's college. Going to perform our choir numbers. We're dressed in blue tee shirts an' jeans. I'm near the back of the bus. Got Cory an' Rapid-Glen behind me, last row. Jeb is opposite me. Sanderson is the guard up front with the driver. The armed guards are in the bus behind us. An' as usual they turn off behind us towards their doughnut an' coffee place. Hard habit to break for them, even on show night.

Means when we get to the college parking lot. We got to wait. Just like at Hoover's.

So, we sit in the parking lot. It's evening. Still hot in the bus. Sanderson an' the driver climb out an' wait outside the bus door. Julia's already outside the bus. Chatting to Sanderson an' the driver.

I hear two clicks from behind me. Jeb an' me look 'round. Cory's got a key in his hand. He's just unlocked his'self an' Rapid-Glen from the chain.

Leans forward to me an' Jeb. Says very quietly we're going to unlock a bunch of us. Wait until I say, then we all storm out. Sanderson can't get us all.

For once I can see a move or two ahead in Cory's chess game. An' I don't like it. An' I see two moves backward. That time when Zabriski had Corey unlock the chain gang an' Cory had a bar of soap. You squeeze the key into the soap. The soap takes the exact shape of the key. Then you give the key back to Zabriski. Later you make a copy of the key from your bar of soap.

Also, that's why Cory wants Rapid-Glen in the choir. The guy who can't sing. The parking lot is huge, a mass of cars for college an' for the choir show. Hundreds an' hundreds. It's a maze to disappear into. Rapid-Glen will have one hot-wired an' running down the highway before you can say JAIL BREAK. The rest of us are just bait to distract Sanderson before the armed guards show up.

Jeb an' me we look at each other. Remind myself that Jeb is a good chess player too. I'm damn sure he's figgered out what I've figgered out. Jeb's big an' mean. But he's no ways dumb. He's looking at me, like he's asking what I think. I give him a small shake of my head.

Jeb says to Cory an' RG – what about Julia?

Rapid-Glen says - I don't care. Knock her down or take her hostage. Hostage might help you get away. Do what you want with her.

RG might be good with cars, but he's way off figgering out Jeb.

Jeb stares at him for a moment. Not a good stare.

Rapid-Glen says – or you can stay in the bus. The rest of us will take care of her. Might take care of her myself.

Cory, now, he's much better at figgering out people. He looks at Jeb, looks at RG an' starts to say something to calm Jeb. He sees what RG doesn't see. Jeb is set to explode.

Cory's waving his hands at Jeb, like he wants to say – back up a moment, I can explain.

But Jeb is too fast. Doesn't let either one talk. Give each one a knock in the gut. Not too gentle, not full force neither. I hear their air whooshing out, hear them wheezing trying to get some breath back, air whistling an' whining in their throats like a half broken vacuum cleaner startin' up. He pushes them back onto the bus bench. Didn't know he was that quick. Quick for even a small guy, never-mind a huge guy like him. Has the chain an' padlocks back on their leg before you can say home run. Two clicks an' they're locked back down. Grabs the home-made key out of Cory's hands. Folds one big dinner-plate hand around the key.

I know why he did all that. Not sure whether Cory had it figgered out yet. Prob'ly not. Cory was too busy trying to breathe. RG, 'course he's clueless about why. An' trying to breathe.

I remember how Sanderson snuck up on me in the library when I was looking at women on the internet. Damn me, if he hasn't done it again. Not sure how much he saw, but now he's standing at the bench in front of me an' Jeb saying – do we have a problem, boys?

Jeb says – no problem, Boss. Everything's fine.

Never heard Jeb call anyone Boss before. Like he's trying to calm Sanderson.

The two of them look at each other for a long while. Sanderson nods at him, like he's saying – good.

Then he steps closer to Jeb, blocks my view, blocks everyone's view. Not sure ifn' Jeb maybe hands him the key. Can't see. Neither one says anything I can hear. I know I never see the key again.

Sanderson steps back an' says to Jeb – they gonna be OK to sing? He's looking at Cory an' RG.

Jeb says – yes Boss, it's just allergy. Pollen in the air. They'll be fine when they're indoors. I'll make sure they're good to sing.

I think to myself. That's why he pulled his punches. His normal punch would have killed them both.

Sanderson nods. Looks one more time at the padlocks on our legs an' walks back out of the bus. Cool as ifn' nothing happened.

RG an' Cory have kind of got their breath back by

now.

RG says – what the fuck you doing Jeb? Don't you wanna get out of Dildo?

More a wheeze than real talking. Like he's imitating the Godfather movie. Still, you get what he's saying.

Jeb says to him, real low – I got a daughter. Won't speak to me because I let her down. Because I'm a con. Reminds me of Miss Julia. Might think they were twins if you didn't know. Like two peas. Not going to let another one down. So you better sing tonight. Real good. If you don't your allergy is going to get real serious after. We clear?

RG goes paler still an' nods.

Jeb turns to Cory. Says – you too. You going to sing better than ever. Or your allergy will kill you. We clear?

Cory nods. Says – I'm clear.

Cory's just lost a chess game to a better player. He looks real tired. His plans for getting out or over for now. His worries about Gracia are back. Bigger than ever.

Ten minutes later turns out maybe Jeb did him a big favour. The bus with the rifle guards shows up. Sanderson unlocks our chains an' we get out. Then we see the guards with the sidearms. They came separately from the rifle guards. The guys with the sidearms were standing outside with Sanderson an' Julia right from the start. Just we didn't see them. Blocked by the height of the bus. An' Cory didn't reckon on them being there. Would have gotten real ugly ifn' we had tried escaping the bus.

We end up giving a great choir show. Sing like we'd never sung before. The audience loves us. Lots of stomping, clapping an' whistling in the audience. Long applause after each number. I hear the TV audience loved it too. Shame it was for a local channel only. Most of the choir have family that would've been proud to see us.

The Warden is our MC. Does a good job. 'Course he would. He's a born politician that one. Smooth as goose shit an' twice as slippery. The TV folk love him.

An' after the show all the college brass get in front of the TV cameras too, the college president, dean of the music faculty, dean of the arts, whatever. Everyone wants to tell the TV audience how great this evening was – an' how important he or she was in making it happen.

The Dean of Arts, now there's a women who might give the Warden a run for goose poop. Woman by the name of Dr. Denneman. Not the kind of doctor that can set broken bones. The other kind. Had nothing much to do with anything tonight, but she's in front of the cameras giving a long speech about her department's history of finding the artistic genius buried within the downtrodden an' overlooked. She says this is a core of her philosophy, something that she instills in even the most junior of her students – gives a small nod to Julia - and has shaped the history of the theatre under her tenure.

Whatever that is. For a while I'm understanding ten year, not tenure. Was scared she was going to keep talking for ten years. The camera crew finally wander away an' that shuts her up. She's not happy. She's even less happy that the camera crew spend more time interviewing Julia than her. I watch the Dean, her mouth tightens, wrinkles like a dried up apple, an' she gets a mean look. Gonna be trouble with that one.

One little change before we first started singing. Norm'ly Jeb stands with the bass section. This time he put his'self behind the tenors. Right behind Cory an' Rapid-Glen.

Julia looks at him an' raises an eyebrow. Like – what you doing over there? He looks at her an' mouths something I don't get. She gives a tiny shoulder shrug. Doubt the audience even noticed. Anyhows, Julia lets it go. Lets him stand where he wants.

She's always given Jeb a little slack. Not because he's big. Heck, she ain't scared of big. Seems to me she ain't scared of hardly anything. An' she doesn't know about what happened on the bus. No-one but Cory, RG, Jeb, an' me know about that. Sanderson knows a bit, don't know how much. But no one else knows. Ever. Part is Jeb's such a good singer. The other part, tell you what, I reckon she gives him slack because of the way he acts towards her. Like a big mother bear around its cub.

But Cory an' Rapid-Glen know why he's standing behind them. They sing real loud an' clear. Maybe not as tuneful as always, but real loud.

44. Ratshit

You'd think after our great concert an' all the excitement from the Warden, local TV, the college, the audience an' all we'd be set for more shows. Maybe national TV. Maybe a recording contract. Fame. Sponsorships by Nike an' Coke. Interviews on the Late Night Show. Money. An Emmy. Early parole.

That's not how a con's life works. Ifn' we don't screw it up for ourselves, someone else will.

Our lives are ruled by a misery meter. The rule is the average reading on the misery meter cannot change. That means ifn' you have an up day, like a great concert at the college, you have to have some down days after. When everything turns to ratshit. So that the average for the misery meter still points to miserable.

I see the signs early. The college arts an' music department starts messing with Julia. Lots of big words that I wouldn't know ifn' Julia hadn't told us. What with my memr'y being what it is I can repeat them. I can tell the words mean they're messing with her. Words like - need for formalization, need for standardization, curricular relevance, deviation from standards, uncalibrated security risks, checkpoints, validation, lack of senior oversight, need for senior oversight, need for senior programme planning an' programme management, lack of dean's approval, unauthorized press an' TV contacts by a junior student without reference to college communications framework, junior students exceeding a student-appropriate role, lack of senior sign-off, might be better off back in the chemistry department where independent research is encouraged.

Now just maybe ifn' Cory's heart was still in it, he an' Julia would have figgered out how to get around that piece of politics. But Cory's heart is no longer in it. That chess game is over for him. Doesn't even want to sing any more. 'Sides which Cory's got some medical problem now with his foot. Rapid-Glen doesn't want to sing any more. Though in his case that'd make the choir sound better. Hubbard can't sing any more – he's away sitting in a hospital with his wife somewhere. An' the news ain't good. I hear she's in a coma.

Two other choir members get in a fight with each other an' get put in solitary. One other choir member finally comes up for parole an' leaves prison. That's half our choir missing in action.

Julia explains some of this stuff to us at the Sunday after our big concert. It's rehearsal time for the choir. At Dildo Correctional. But we don't rehearse. It's meant to be a celebration of our concert success. Julia lays on cake an' some fizzy drink that's meant to be like champagne with no alcohol. Thanks us for all our work. Tells us how great we were. Says it's beyond anything she expected from us.

But.

The choir is on hold for now. This will be the last Sunday choir meeting for now. The Warden an' the Dean of Arts, that's Dr. Denneman, the lady with the mouth like an old prune, have to sort out who's doing what. Who's going to mop up any TV publicity down the road. Who's going to mop up any money or sponsorship. Which prof or dean will replace Julia as a choir master. Soak up the glory. Watch this space. Stay tuned.

45. Cory on Light Duty

Cory comes back from Hoover's one day, limping. Got a septic cut an' a huge infection in the sole of his foot. Don't know how you cut the underside of your foot while wearing boots. Makes me wonder whether Cory has another chess game starting. For sure though the foot is bad. Even the useless medic admits it's serious. Gives Cory antibiotics an' says he has to be on light duty where he doesn't have to stand or walk.

McCreedy is the duty officer that day. Puts Cory down for work in the clerk's office until further notice.

Man, oh man. That's dumb. That's like the time McCreedy tried to force me to eat meat. Putting Cory, the master forger, near official documents? That's like putting crocodiles to work in the kindergarten.

46. Hubbard

Hubbard comes back. He's in a bad way. His wife didn't make it. I ask Mrs. Haverman in the library to let Julia know. Figger she'd want to know. Even though the choir is on hold while the college an' the prison sort out who's on first base.

Julia comes to visit Hubbard the very next day. Not sure how she got to see him. It is visitors' day, but she's not on the list of approved visitors for Hubbard. Guess she bulldozed her way in the way she bulldozed us into being a choir. They talk for a long time. Not sure what they say. Julia comes out with her face all twisted. Near runs back to the parking lot. Doesn't want to talk to anyone else. Think she didn't want anyone to see her cry. Wanted to get to her car as quickly as possible before she started to howl. She's just found out the hardest way there are things she an' music can't cure. Things she can't bulldoze right. She's really upset. Hubbard got there too late. His wife had slipped into a coma before he got there. While he was still on the train. His wife didn't know he was there. Didn't speak a word to him. Didn't hear a word from him. Died as though she's alone. Abandoned.

Julia tells her Mom she never wants to see inside a prison again. Never wants to be near a prison again. Mrs. H. breaks the news to me the next day. Mrs. H. says Julia cried all night.

The next week at Hoover's Hubbard picks up a big rock an' takes a run straight at the armed guards. Waving the rock at them an' shouting. Figger he was wanting to end it all with a quick rifle bullet. Suicide by guard an' rifle. Of course his chain doesn't have enough slack in it to get to the guards. He was hoping they'd shoot him by reflex. They don't. Just take the rock away from him an' put him in protective custody. After that Hubbard is reclassified as needing a higher security detention facility than Dildo. He's shipped out of Dildo two days later an' I never hear from him again. Wisht I knew where he was, an ifn' he's OK.

47. Reaction

The cons take the news about Hubbard different ways. The long-timers have seen this kind of thing too often. They know not to react. No point. The new comers are shaken. Hiero is angry. Says – if they didn't waste three days making him fill out forms, he'd have got to her. Spoken to her. Told her he was there for her. Before she dropped into a coma.

Never thought Hiero could get angry. He's always so quiet. Even after what they done to him he wasn't real angry. This time he's spitting mad.

An' Julia never coming back. The cons take that news different ways too.

Jeb rights a note to her saying thank you for all you've done. Writes he hopes she'll be OK. Never thought Jeb could write. Real neat hand too. Asks me to pass the letter to Mrs. Haverman. For her to give Julia. Technically that's smuggling. Mrs. H passes on the letter anyways.

The long-time cons shrug. They knew in their bones this choir thing couldn't last. Was too much fun. Against the rules of the misery meter.

Slow Joey though takes it hard. Comes to me 'bout three days in a row. Same question each day.

Says – Pango, is she going to come back?

I say – don't think so, Joey.

He goes away looking upset an' like he don't understand. Comes back again the next day. Same question. 'Til I shout at him. Then I feel bad, an' try an' explain it again slowly. Still don't think he really understands.

48. Cory Again

I'm chatting to Cory in the exercise yard. He's on at me about a cough I've got. Dunno why.

Says to me – You've had that even before you worked the gravel pit. Got worse in the gravel pit, an' you still got it.

I say – Whatever.

Cory says – It's a pain at night when the rest of us are trying to sleep. Can't sleep because we're listening to you hacking away.

News to me. I generally hear Cory sawing wood long before I get to sleep.

He's not letting up though.

Says – Pango, I know I owe you big time. For lots you've done for me. But you owe me too. For when I got Will Sorrel to back off jousting you.

This is not how Cory norml'y acts with me. Not sure what he's up to.

So? – I say.

So – he says – I want you to book an appointment with the medic. My payback for Will Sorrel.

The medic hates me – I say – almost got disbarred for near letting me die. When I wasn't eating.

That's why he'll be extra careful in examining you this time.

Takes weeks to get an appointment – I say.

The sooner you make it. The sooner you get it.

I look at him a while. Trying to figger what his angle is now. Cory's a master poker player though. Face doesn't show a thing. Should have known it wouldn't.

Do it – he says.

OK – I say.

49. Zabriski

While the misery meter is dropping, we do actually win a small battle.

There's an inspection back at our dorm. Zabriski's pissed that he wasn't on TV, wasn't MC at our big do. Shows it when it's his turn to do our early morning dorm inspection. Lines us up at our beds an' puts on white cotton gloves.

He's done that a few times in the past when he's pissed. Runs his fingers over railings an' window sills an' in cracks in the mortar. Any dust shows up black on his gloves. Then we lose privileges. The whole dorm. So today he puts on white gloves. Goes to each con in turn.

Says – did you clean an' dust around your bed?

The cons say – yes, Sir.

We've kinda been expecting this. We talked about it after the big concert. Every one of us said - Zabriski looks pissed. Gonna take it out on us. Gonna have a white glove inspection for sure.

So we've done extra cleaning. Zabriski checks. With gloves on. Things look good an' clean. 'Till Zabriski gets to Low Dog.

Zabriski says – did you clean?

LD says – yes, Sir.

Zabriski runs his fingers over an' under LD's bed frame. So far so good. Then he looks at the barred window off to one side of LD's bed. Says to LD – did you wipe an' clean the window frame an' the bars?

LD says – no, Sir.

Zabriski runs his gloved finger over the bars anyway.

His glove is still clean. He's not happy. Wants to find something. Runs his finger over the bottom of the window frame. His glove stays clean. He's not happy.

I'm watching him with one eye an' LD with another.

LD, that balanced personality who has no issues with authority. At least according to Parker, the anger management idiot.

Parker should have asked me ifn' I was angry at him. At Parker. Would've said, yes. Idiots who set themselves up as experts always make me angry. Idiots who poke at caged dogs make me angry. But that's the question Parker didn't think to ask. 'Cause he's not an expert.

Anyhows, I can tell that LD's up to something. He's wound up. Like a kid waiting for Christmas morning.

Then Zabriski reaches way up to the top part of the window frame. There's a line of brick up there. They stick out from the wall in a line across the window top. Make an upper window sill. Zabriski can't see what's up there, on top of the bricks, but his fingers can reach. Seems to me LD is holding his breath. Zabriski sweeps two gloved fingers across the top sill.

An' shouts like a stuck pig.

He's pulls back his hand from up there like it was hot stove. Real quick. One moment his fingers are sweeping across the top sill. Before I know it his hand is down, level with his gut. He's gripping the two fingers with is other hand. There's blood dripping from his two fingers. A deep cut across each fingertip. The glove is soaking up the blood, getting redder an' redder. First the two fingers, then the other fingers, then the palm.

Finally gets his cursing an' shock under control. Manages to slow the bleeding by pressure with the other hand. Picks on a con called Arnie. Arnie's a young guy.

Big arm muscles. Always doing pull-ups in the exercise yards. Even one-arm pull-ups.

Says to Arnie – pull yourself up by the window bars an' see what the hell is atop there.

Arnie pulls his'self up, gets his feet on the bottom sill. Reaches for something up there an' pulls it down. Climbs back down an' holds it out for Zabriski to see.

A small piece of metal. You can see it used to be a long thin cylinder. Maybe three inches long. Someone's flattened the cylinder along one long side, hammered it flat, an' sharpened the flat bit. Like a razor blade.

The young con says - This was stuck up there, in the mortar, Sir. Sharp end facing up.

Zabriski is close to hitting Low Dog.

Low Dog says – don't know nothin' about that, Sir. I didn't clean up there. Must be from the old days when this was an army camp. Once we found a nine mill bullet under the dorm.

Which is true. About five years ago.

Zabriski knows he's been outwitted. No way he can prove Low Dog put the blade up there. An' played him for a sucker. Ifn' Low Dog said he'd cleaned up there it'd be different. But Low Dog said in front of twenty witnesses he didn't clean up there.

Tries things a few different ways with Low Dog.

Says to him – So why didn't you clean up there?

LD says – can't reach, Sir. I'm way too short.

I think to myself – No, but you climbed up the window bars last night, just like Arnie did now. I saw. An' that home-made blade looks like it was made from the missing swill bin hinge. An' you've been on swill bin duty a fair whack this month.

Of course none of us says anything like this to

Zabriski. We all look surprised. Or blank.

Zabriski says to LD – so why don't you put a bed or something underneath the window to stand on?

Realizes as soon as he says it, it's dumb.

LD doesn't crack a smile.

Just says, like it wasn't a dumb question – our beds an' stuff are all bolted down, Sir. Can't move 'em, Sir.

Worst Zabriski can do is take away privileges from all of us. Which is what he does. For not having a clean window sill. Where many of us can't reach anyway.

Before he's done though he looks across all our faces. Trying to figger out who else was in on this. Stops in front of Jeb. Says – you laughing, boy?

Zabriski will call any of us boy. Black, white, brown, red or yellow. It's to show he's the man an' we're not.

Jeb's face has been blank all along. As best I can tell. It's just Zabriski trying to stir up stuff.

No, Sir – says Jeb.

Zabriski gives him a long look. Says – I've got my eye on you, boy. I'm not finished with you either.

Then walks out. Going to get his fingers bandaged.

The guys walk over to Low Dog an' slap his hand or pat his back. One small triumph for the cons.

Cory nods at Low Dog. Even in Cory's books this is a good one.

50. Sanderson an' Jeb

Something that comes out of the near escape on the bus is Sanderson an' Jeb are kind of buddies now. Not that guards an' cons are ever real buddies. But they'll nod to each other. Not much, but more than guards an' cons norm'ly do. Sanderson will nod an' say – g'day Jeb.

Like Jeb's a real person, not just a con. A person with a real name. Jeb.

Jeb'll nod back an' say – day Officer Sanderson, Sir.

That, an' the bad blood between Sanderson an' Zabriski might explain what happened out at Hoover's farm.

We're digging away in the heat. Sanderson an' Zabriski both are near where Jeb is digging. Hiero is next on the chain to Jeb. Digging. We're doing some kind of singing to keep the rhythm. Not a real song. Just a chant that cons at Dildo have been using for years.

Lift that pick - Lift

Ugh

Drop that pick - Drop

Ugh

Swing it free - Swing

Ugh

Work's all shit – Shit

Ugh

Life's no good – Good

Ugh

An' so on.

As usual at Hoover's Jeb doesn't sing. Just grunts.

We pause while another team is pulling a tree stump out of the ditch we have to dig. We step back, leave our shovels an' picks over at the ditch.

I can tell Zabriski is still pissed at us. Starts messing with Jeb.

Says – How come you not singing, pretty boy? You sang OK in the choir.

Jeb says – Don't sing at work, Sir.

Zabriski steps closer with his damn dog. Let's the dog get real close to Jeb. Dog is growling.

Says – Maybe my dog can persuade you to sing – maybe make you sing real high.

He's pointing his finger at Jeb's face. Getting real close

Jeb looks at the dog. Doesn't know which of the two he should deal with. Feels crowded having to deal with both. Has his fists up ready to defend against either, an' to keep Zabriski's finger out of his face.

Then out of nowhere. Surprises us all. Hiero. On the chain next to Jeb. Seems to know about dogs. Steps forward to the dog. Says in this loud voice – SIT!

Damn me, to hell an' back. Says it in a voice that makes my skull ring. Real angry voice. Still angry about Hubbard I guess. Echoes in my head an' down to my boots. So angry, I nearly damn sat too. Think the whole chain gang nearly sat. Prob'ly a few guards nearly sat. Hard not to. The dog sure sat. Straight off. Like it was caught lifting sausage off the toddler's plate.

Looked at Hiero, like it was saying – I'm sitting! I'm sitting! Don't beat me! I'll never take sausage from the baby again! I'm a bad dog! I know! Ears drooping. Tail between its legs.

Zabriski is taken by surprise. Things are happening

too quick for him. He's now got Jeb's fists near his face an' no dog to protect him. He brings his own fists up an' steps back one pace.

Drops like a brick.

Ends up on his knees throwing up.

Things happened so quick I have to replay in my head what my eyes just done told me. Replay it twice to make sure I got it right.

Did Sanderson just hit Zabriski with his billy club?

Sanderson is leaning over Zabriski, apologizing. Holding Zabriski's arm so that Zabriski won't fall over further.

Zabriski is saying – What ... what the heck ...?

Sanderson's trying to explain – I was swinging my club to help you an' you stepped back at the wrong moment. You walked back into my club.

Zabriski is throwing up again. Looking down at the ground with his mouth wide open. Can't see that Sanderson an' Jeb are looking at each other. Doesn't see Sanderson looking at Jeb. Half closing his eyes. Not quite a wink. Almost. Doesn't see Jeb half nod back at him. Just the tiniest head movement. A tiny lift to the corner of his mouth. Not a smile. But the beginnings. You had to be standing real close to notice. Ifn' you'd have blinked you'd have missed it.

An' I'm remembering how Zabriski cursed Sanderson an' Valerie in the parking lot, an' how Jeb locked up Cory an' Rapid-Glen on the bus. Now I'm sure. Sanderson knows about the bus. He saw it all.

After that there's a big ruckus. Zabriski gets sent home, still feeling dizzy. The dog follows him. Still dragging its tail between its legs. Ready to sit. Instantly. Ifn' Hiero even clears his throat. Keeps looking back at

Hiero.

Jeb gets led off in cuffs an' ankle chains. Gets put in solitary pending a big enquiry. I expect the guards to beat on him after they march him away. For solidarity. They don't. Guess they don't like Miss Charm, Officer Zabriski, neither.

The Special Response Team roars up loaded for bear an' find nothing but us guys doing our regular digging. Roar off again, looking real let down. All dressed up an' nobody to shoot.

At the enquiry Sanderson explains again how he's swinging his club free of his belt. Just in case things get ugly. An' Zabriski steps back into it.

There's talk of charging Jeb. Criminal charges. Sanderson testifies Jeb put up his hands because of the Zabriski an' the dog. Threatening him because he wouldn't sing. Warden pops a fuse at Zabriski. Pops another one because of the damn dog. That's not prison procedure. Undermines any criminal charges he might have brought against Jeb, that an' the damn fool singing business.

Zabriski tries to spin the story differently. Tells the Warden Jeb was going to attack him. His word against Sanderson. Jeb's word doesn't count –he's a con. One of the armed guards steps forward. Backs up Sanderson's story, word perfect. Surprises me a bit. Seems to have seen a lot of detail for someone standing 5 yards back. Lights go on later. I hear he's Valerie's brother.

Zabriski tries one more defense. Doesn't realize the Warden isn't in the mood. Tries to say how Hiero told his dog to sit. Why isn't Hiero on charge too? Warden gets purple in the face. Reams out Zabriski for 5 minutes solid. Says if Zabriski says one more word, Warden will put him an' his dog together in solitary right now. Without food.

Until one of them eats the other. An' Warden hopes it's the dog that gets the last meal. Ifn' Zabriski survives Warden says he'll put the dog collar on Zabriski until Zabriski learns to sit when Hiero tells him. An' Warden never wants to see that dog again.

Norm'ly wouldn't talk like that to a guard in front of a con. But Jeb is there as part of the enquiry. An' the Warden is plenty riled.

I hear most of this from Jeb. After he gets out of solitary.

Warden gives Jeb 15 day's solitary anyhow. Which is getting off light, considering.

Gives Zabriski an official reprimand an' loss of five day's pay for incompetence. An' for calling in the Special Response Team. Makes sarcastic comments about dumb guards that need the SRT because a con won't sing.

Sanderson gets a reprimand too. Warden reams him out for being careless with his club.

Sanderson says – yes, Sir. Very sorry, Sir.

He's very careful. Doesn't look once at Jeb throughout. Jeb doesn't look once at him. Funny thing that. Would have stood out a mile to any con watching. Cory could have told you what that means. But Warden doesn't notice.

51. Strawberries an' Cream

Round about then we needed any laughs we could get. Us cons were still feeling pretty raw about Hubbard. An' losing our choir master. An' even though we got two up on Zabriski, those were near things. Might have turned ugly. Nearly did. Might still. Trust Matthew to bring a grin at the right time.

Food at Dildo Correctional is as bad as you'd think. An' boring. No variety. But one Christmas, a local supermarket chain decides to do a charity drive for the Dildo prisoners. It donates money an' food for a special Christmas dinner for the cons. Don't know how or why they picked on us. We're not the most worthy cause out there at Christmas time. Sure appreciated it though. Was really good.

The part us cons talked about for months after was dessert. Fresh strawberries with whipped cream. We rarely see fresh fruit. An' never strawberries. An' never fresh whipped cream. Prob'ly the best meal I had in seven years inside. There were cons who didn't want to give up their empty bowls. Even when they'd scraped out every last drop of cream an' every last strawberry seed. Sat their staring at the bowls. As though maybe they'd spot another smear of cream or strawberry juice. Ifn' they just kept looking long enough.

So months after that dessert, Matthew is on swill duty. Happens to be on the inside of the locked back gate when the pig farmer is driving by on the outside. On a tractor with a truck load behind. Truck load of something that smells downright evil.

Matthew says – Hey – farmer man - what's that in the

truck. Smells like ripe sheeyit.

Farmer says – Hey old feller. It is. It's manure.

Matthew says – What you doing with it?

Farmer says – Gonna put it on my strawberries.

Matthew says – You should come eat here with us. We put cream on ours.

52. Crocodile in the Kindergarten

Cory's foot has healed up nicely. He's back working the chain gang with the rest of us when his letter arrives in the Warden's office. It's a sentence reduction under Section 5K1.1 of the US Sentencing Guidelines and Rule 35.

Us cons smell a Cory fraud. Cory shakes his head. Tells us we're too suspicious. Which doesn't mean a thing. It's what he'd say either way.

For sure the prison clerk's office checks back with the court clerk an' all. Everything comes up smelling roses on that side too. Ifn' it's a fake letter, the fake has a twin copy in the court records. Don't know how Cory pulled this stunt.

For all that the letter appears real, it doesn't add up. Section 5K1.1 an' all that. I'm no lawyer, but that's sentence reduction in return for a con co-operating with an investigation. Cory's no snitch. Us cons will swear that. An' what investigation?

Anyhows, Dildo Correctional is in a real hurry to let him go. According to his sentence reduction he should have been out a week ago. Some delay in the paperwork means the letter arrives late at Dildo. Now prison admin scurries to get him released. Takes two more days an' it's all set up.

I have time for just a few questions for Cory. We're alone.

I say – you going back to printing money?

He says – No, Pango. Times have changed. The scams now are online, electronic, computerized, digital. Big money resides in digital records an' zeros an' ones. I got skills in those directions too. Might surprise you. Have contacts with those skills too. Might use them, combined with my skills. Paper money is small change these days. An' too easy to track. Tracking fake zeros an' ones is hard.

We shake hands him an' me. Seems just minutes after that I see he's outside in the parking lot with Gracia ready to drive him away.

I feel like I've been hit by an earthquake. Cory's bin here long as I have. Now he's gone. Hubbard's gone. Zabriski's damn dog is gone. Julia's gone. Our choir rehearsals are gone. Jeb an' Sanderson - a guard an' a con - are saying good morning to each other. An' the metal shop oven is brewing balm of Gilead most weekends. For the first time in seven years seems like a lot of stuff is suddenly moving on from me. Running away from me. Like the ground moving in a quake. An' I don't like it. After seven years these changes are getting to me. Can't handle 'em the way I could when I was a real person on the outside.

Cory's leaving reminds me of my promise. I book an appointment with the medic. Like Cory said, the medic is all kid gloves. Does it all by the book. Doesn't want to be shown up again over how he treats me. Actually sees me the next week - not a long wait at all. Listens to my lungs an' orders all kinds of tests to cover his ass. X-rays up my ying yang, ultrasounds, blood tests an' such like. Words I can't pronounce. He says a week an' he'll let me know the results.

53. Any Complaints?

Another change. The biggest of all. Actually two changes.

The first is I go back to the medic when the results come in. I expect he's gonna hold up those big old black an' white x-ray sheets. The ones you hold to the window so the light can shine through from behind. Nope. The test results are all sitting on his computer. Like Cory warned me the world is digital.

The medic stares at his computer. Tells me he's consulted with specialists. The x-rays an' what all show lumps in my lungs that have spread to other major organs. Spread too far an' fast for him to think of treatment. The specialists agree. He's recommending my urgent release on compassionate grounds. Says I should go home to family. Talks some more 'bout options an' pain management. Mainly what I hear is I might have six months, might have a year.

An' before I can get my head around that part, the release is granted. Actually takes about four weeks. That's lightning by prison standards. Before I'm ready for the change, Dildo gives me back the civvy suite I wore to court, gives me a sandwich, gives me money from my account, makes me sign a whack of forms, asks me ifn' I have any complaints, an' opens the doors.

The question about complaints, they always ask that when a con leaves. Of course, no con wants to delay leaving by saying yes. Would lead to who knows how many days of enquiry an' how many more forms. Cons always say – No.

Mrs. Haverman shuts the library special. So as she

can come down to say goodbye. Says she will miss me, an' I should write to her. Gives me a hug. Says Julia sends her best wishes. Tells me I was one of Julia's favourites. An' Julia also says I should write. Then she says – I have a present for you.

Gives me a book. I recognize it straight off.

She says – It's legal. I've been deleting books from the library that no one uses. This is no longer library property. It's for you.

It's "The Child's Book of Victorian Parlour Games", 1878-1888, Volume 3, By Edgar G. Greenlock, reprinted 1907 by Jonathan Harper an' Sons.

How did you know? – I say

I know more than you think – she says.

Did you read it? – I ask.

No – she says – after I saw you were putting your diary pages in this, it was private. I never read it.

You didn't mind that I was tearing out real book pages to make space for my diary?

No – she says – I thought a diary might be more valuable than a list of long forgotten parlour games. I knew you couldn't keep a diary safe in the dorm or anywhere else.

Would have liked to give her a hug again, but cons can't do that to staff.

Just say – Mam, thank you. Take care of yourself, an' Julia, an' your Ma.

They open the doors an' it's unconditional. No parole officer. No reporting to police stations. They know from my record that there's no chance I'll reoffend. No way to repeat the one crime that brought me here. Impossible.

They ask me ifn' I want to book a taxi or call my daughter or son.

I say no. I'll walk, hitch-hike, or take a bus, an' take some time to think how I'm going to tell my kids. Is it good news? Or bad? I don't rightly know what to tell them. Fraid' to tell them I'm sick. They're good kids. Don't need this trouble of mine. Had enough trouble on my account.

Claire, that's my daughter, an' her hubby have young Jonathon to look after. Fourteen months old. That's a handful. Gregory, my son, is studying to pass another of the banking exams as he moves up the ladder in the bank. Works hard by day. Studies at night. Trying to make as much of his skills an' life as he can. Not much free time.

By now they're used to me being a con. Come to terms with that. Not used to me being a dying father they need to take in. On top of everything.

Got to take a day or two before I call. I'm no good anymore at making decisions or thinking fast. After seven years I'm like Slow Joey. Going to take some time before I'm really ready for what's happening to me.

Another thing. I'm walking down a road. Free man. But. I still feel I'm a con. Can't seem to shake that name for myself. I try saying to my self – Pango, you're a real person, free, outside, real world.

Doesn't sound right. 'Nother voice in my head says – Pango, you're a con.

Almost want to turn back to the Dildo gates an' say – wait, take me back.

54. The Road

Once out of the Deep South, our route northwards took us through Tennessee, Virginia, Maryland, Pennsylvania and into New England.

Somewhere near Knoxville, Tennessee, Pango bought himself a cell phone during a lunch stop. That evening he had a long conversation with each of his kids. I hadn't yet heard his full story. I did know he had been released on medical grounds and had been hesitating on how to break the news.

After his phone calls he looked relieved. He told me his kids were happy he was out, happy he was coming to see them. All three agreed to put the medical issues aside for now. Claire said "let's first celebrate the reunion. Let's not even think of the health issues. Live for the day."

Pango was clearly relieved. He'd worried about being a burden on his kids. Instead, they were excited at his release. He smiled more after that call.

"Funny", he said to me. "Way back when, Cory he told me I was too serious. Told me he would teach me to live for the day. But it's Claire that's teaching me.

She's saying 'Dad, live for the day'".

For all that he was keen now to see Claire, he was good natured when I stopped for photography along the way. I had a new Sony mirrorless, with a bunch of Zeiss glass, and was enjoying working with them. Pango helped me with tripods and lugging extra lenses. Occasionally I still pulled out a big, heavy medium format and its lenses and he always volunteered to help me carry the load. He had a good eye for natural scenery and often as not he would point out possibilities that I had overlooked.

55. Maine

My plan was to drop Pango off at Claire's and then to move on. I thought I'd leave them to a long overdue celebration. Just Pango, Claire and her family. It didn't work out like that.

Claire had Jonathon in one arm, her other wrapped tightly around Pango while directing me into the kitchen for coffee.

I said – "Well OK, thanks, if it's not a problem, just a coffee, then I'll leave you to it".

Somehow before coffee was done, supper appeared.

So I said – "Well thanks, sure, if it's not a problem."

Pango had taken me aside after the second cup of coffee and asked that I stayed a bit. He said it bothered him in Dildo people disappeared without notice. Like Hubbard, like Cory, like Julia. Gone before you knew it.

He said – We been together on the road five days. Talked a lot. Shared some stories. Yours an' mine both. Don't want to see you just disappear. Would seem like I hadn't had a chance to show appreciation. Wouldn't seem right. Stay for a while. Claire an' Everett are the same mind. They want a chance to say thank you for bringing me all this way.

Claire's husband, Everett, also had taken me aside when the others were out of the room and given me the same message with a different twist. Everett is a quiet, soft spoke trawler captain, used to judging trawler crews in good times and bad, and perhaps as good an intuitive student of human nature, as I've ever met. He'd summed up one of Pango's needs as supper was arriving.

He said to me "it would be good for Pango, if you

could stay for a few days with us. He's used to inmates being treated like me and my crew treat a fish catch. In bulk. Catch them by the hundreds. Sort them by the hundreds. Pour them onto ice. Store them in the hold. Offload them at the dock. By the hundreds. He needs to learn to be treated as an individual again. He's taken a shine to you. If you have the time stay with us a while before you move on it might show him that he's not being processed in bulk anymore. That he's not a faceless hitchhiker being picked up on the road, dropped off and forgotten. Claire and I, we'd be tickled to have you stay, if you can. If you can't, if you've got places you need to be, of course we understand. You've already been plenty generous in bringing him all the way. Don't want you to feel railroaded. Just saying, if you've got a mind to stay for a few days, we'd love to have you."

Supper went on until near midnight with Claire and Pango mostly talking, but sometimes just beaming sideways at each other or down at sleeping Jonathan. When she wasn't eating or dishing up Claire would sit with one hand holding onto her father's arm or hand.

He said – She used to hang on to my hand at meals when she was little. When I came home from a ship. Her Ma would say 'let your Pa eat in peace'. Then she'd let go my hand an' make this sad face. 'Til I said 'it's OK honey. You hang onto my hand ifn' you want to.' Learned to eat with one hand. Still can.

He put an arm around her while she leaned close.

Claire had prepared a huge vegetarian chili. Everett had baked fresh bread for the occasion. She opened some white wine. Everett and I had some beer with the chili. Pango tasted first the wine, then the beer, and shook his head.

He said ruefully – looks like I've lost the taste for

these. The wine tastes sour an' the beer is kind of bitter. Didn't really miss them when I was in Bilbo. Wouldn't mind some tea or more coffee ifn' I can get a spoon of sugar with them.

He made an effort to call it Bilbo, but slipped up a couple of times. When Claire and Everett started laughing at the nickname, he gave up and reverted to openly calling it Dildo Erection Facility.

He said - When Jonathan is old enough to understand I'll clean up the language.

It was an easy conversation to be a guest at. Claire is a warm-hearted extrovert. She was happy to have her father within reach. Everett is a much quieter personality, giving his wife plenty of room to lead the conversation, occasionally nodding or chiming in with a word here or there. And Claire never let her extroversion overlook others. If Everett was quiet for too long she'd say to him – "Why don't you tell Dad about Jonathon's first words?" or some such topic. A good match for each other.

Claire wanted to know about my photography. She said "there's lots of coastal scenery around here you'd love. We'll show you. If the weather's calm you might even want to go out with the trawler. Take some photos of the guys winching in the nets."

Before I knew it my bags were in a spare room for what I assumed would be just a night or two, but turned out to be a week.

Somehow I'd become part of the family the celebration.

56. Maia

The next morning Everett went off to his trawler while the rest of us – with Jonathan in a stroller - went downtown. Pango, Claire and Jonathan went to find more clothes for Pango. He'd picked up a few tee-shirts and jeans on the road with me, but needed more. I needed to replace a lost lens cap and a camera strap that had frayed.

In the afternoon Claire and Everett were working while Jonathan spent the afternoon at Everett's parents. Pango and I brewed coffee back at Claire and Everett's house and relaxed.

It was a typical New England house – clapboard siding, steep roof to shed snow, a central stone chimney - all meticulously kept and set on a small lawn overlooking the Atlantic. Inside Claire and Everett had created a feeling of quiet warmth. Large modern triple glaze windows let light reflect off pale yellow maple floors, white walls, blue trim, and dark wood furniture. In the living room we sat back in soft armchairs with views onto the water. The walls were decorated with family photos and trawling photos. There was a wind whipping up froth on the waves outside and we were both, I think, happy to sit inside and to be lazy after so many days on the road.

Was that you and your wife? – I asked Pango – pointing to a framed black and white of a younger Pango with his arm around a young woman.

He gazed at the photo, smiling as he looked at her.

Yes – he said – that's Maia, my wife.

How did you meet her? – I asked. In our lazy, relaxed mood I guessed he be open for some more yarning.

Oh- said – Pango – I owe that to a senator by the name of Wesley Jones. For a while even considered naming my son Wesley, in his honour. Don't suppose you've heard tell of Senator Jones or of something called cabotage?

No – I said.

No – said Pango – unless you're a sailor you'd never know. Cabotage is when you ship things between ports in the same country. Back in 1920 Senator Jones an' the US government passed a law to say that for shipping things between US ports the ships had to be US ships. An' crewed by US citizens like me. That law still exists.

Came in real handy for me years and years after that. I'd spent some time sailing out of Australia on cattle ships. Then international shipping got bad for a spell. Ships sat in dock empty. Going nowhere. Hard to find work. 'Cause of the Jones act I found coastal shipping work back here in the US. Cabotage at first. Ended up on a salvage tug that put into Portland here. The tug needed refits, so the crew got paid off. The skipper asked me to stay on. He wanted someone to sleep aboard while the tug was in dock. Kinda' like a night watchman. Didn't have to be there full time. Just had to sleep aboard an' do the rounds once a day. Suited me just fine. Got a bit of pay for it too. I hadn't spent much time ashore for months. Sailors don't spend much money while we're at sea. I had a fair amount stowed away and could take some time ashore. Had a hankering to stroll the streets and watch land folk again. Wanted to see children, women, trees, dogs, cats, gardens, café's, trains, cinemas, baseball games, cars.

One afternoon I was strolling past a chandlery near the docks. Peered through the window out of curiosity. Changed my life in two beats of my heart.

There was a young woman serving a customer. Tall, slim. Could have been a dancer or a gymnast, she stood so straight, moved so smooth. Way she stood, made her seem twice as tall. Black eyes. Never seen eyes so dark. Long black hair. Made me stick my face to the glass. Like a kid at the candy store. Still, I would have moved on 'ventually, I guess. 'Cept, just then, she smiled at the customer she was helping. That smile caught me. Froze me like people are frozen for good in that flash thing on your camera. When you look at the picture years later, they're still frozen. Same look, same position as they were in years ago. That smile was like that. Froze me. Seemed to light up the whole store. Then the two of them turned away from me. The light was gone. Hard to make you understand. Don't often try to explain it. Hardly never. Have you heard of Ouessant?

No – I said. Confused at his change of story – What's a Ouessant?

Well – said Pango – English sailors call it Ushant, French call it Ouessant. An island off the coast of France. Sailed past it more times than I care to count. Reefs and wrecks everywhere. Stormy too. Ifn' you go past at night you used to have to look for the lighthouses.

Nowadays ifn' you sail by there it's a radar an' radio controlled corridor. After a couple of oil tankers too many ran aground, the French set up a control tower. Like at an airport. They make ships check in by radio and give them a course to sail. One that will keep them away from the other ships an' off the rocks. Then they track you by radar and radio. But back then there was no control tower, just these huge lighthouses. Six of them on tiny Ouessant. More lighthouses per square mile than any other place in the world.

Ouessant has a mass of reefs and other small islands

nearby. One of them is Molène. The French matelots taught me:

Qui voit Molène voit sa peine

Qui voit Ouessant voit son sang

Means, ifn' you see Molène you'll feel the pain, ifn' you see Ouessant you'll see your blood.

Ifn' you had the bad luck to be off Ouessant at night in a blow you'd stick your face to the wheelhouse windows an' stare an' stare out. Hold your breath an' pray to every god you'd never believed in. Looking for the light from even just one of the lighthouses to shine your way. Light you up. Tell you where you were in the storm. Let you know you were OK, safe from the rocks, or not.

That was what it was like watching her through the window. Needing to see that smile again. Don't know ifn' you'll get what I'm saying. 'Cause, for sure, I've never needed nothin' like that from any other woman.

I get it – I said.

Pango barely paused – 'ventually, she finished with the customer. I walked in. Walked up to her. Asked to buy the first thing I could see. A set of stupid plastic drinking glasses for Sunday yachties. Six glasses. Had a picture on each. A flamingo with a drinking glass in its hand. Sitting under an umbrella on a beach towel. What a dumb-ass thing to ask her for. Just hadn't thought it through. Felt too embarrassed to say anything after that. Bought the glasses and walked out. Hated the glasses an' how dumb I felt. Threw them into the first trashcan I passed.

Ouch – I said.

Yup – he said. I went back the next day. Took all my courage. Had thought it out a bit better this time round.

See, they had a large book section. Nautical books. Asked her for books about wooden boat building, 'specially canoes and kayaks. Asked her for what books did she recommend? She was ...

He paused and looked at the photograph again. Picked it up, cradled it in his hand.

She was ... Maia... Whoever you were, she tried to help, made you a project, gave you full attention. It wasn't busy in the store that afternoon. We spent a fair whack of time together bent over wooden boat magazines and plans. She even bandaged my knuckles. I'd punched the trashcan when I threw away the dumbass drinking glasses and split the skin. She held my hand and put on the bandages. She held my hand in her left hand, like this. Bandaged it with her right.

Didn't want it to end. 'Cause I figgered nothin' in my life after that moment would ever be better than the way she held my hand.

Reminds me of a dog my Pa had when I was growing up. Used to come to me with a thorn in its paw. I'd take it out, and it would look at me with big doggy eyes and put its paw back into my hand. Didn't want me to let go of its paw. Surprised she didn't laugh at me. Or pat me on the head an' give me a dog biscuit. Prob'ly looked just like that dog.

'Course I didn't tell her I'd punched a garbage can.

Didn't tell her neither that I didn't really want to build a canoe. Heck, I'm handy, I can do that kind of stuff. But a canoe?

Anyhows, come the end of the day, by then she knows I'm an out-of-towner and wants to take me under her wing. There's a museum in town where they're going to have a show on wooden boat building. Not canoes, but some kind of dory. She knows one of the old guys who's putting on the demo. Asks me if I want her to take me and introduce me. We did that the next afternoon. Sat'day afternoon.

One thing led to the next. Don't know what she saw in a plain sailor man, but a month later she was spending most nights with me on the tug boat in the harbour. The refit was waiting on a shipment of engine parts. Wasn't going anywhere in a hurry.

When she wasn't working her day job, Maia portrait painted for society weddings. Painted in oils. Worked off wedding photos. Could make the bride and groom look a lot better on her paintings than how they looked on the wedding photos. She loved the light in the wheelhouse – part reflected up from the water, part from the sky. Moved her easel and whatever portrait she was working on into the wheelhouse. Was real neat about it too. Never a drip of paint on the boards.

I introduced her to the skipper. He wanted to make a fuss about her being aboard. Had the wrong idea of what kind of woman I'd brung aboard. 'Course once he met her he was like everyone who met Maia. Couldn't do enough for her. Told her she could paint anywhere on his tug, even ifn' he never saw me again. Said it two minutes after meeting her. Two minutes after that he said ifn' she married him, he'd fire me an' give her the tug as a wedding present. Think he was only half joking. She made him a small painting of him at the wheel of his tug. Beautiful thing. Gave it to him the next week. Could have asked him for the moon after that, an' he'd have given it to her.

I stayed ashore a year. We were married after the first six months. Best thing that ever happened to a dumb-ass sailor like me. Don't know what she saw in me. Marrying a sailor's no easy thing. He's gone half the time. Didn't get easier for her when the kids came along.

I saw a lot of other married sailors. Tried to learn from their mistakes.

Some things were easy. I was never tempted by any other woman when I went ashore somewhere. Never looked at or wanted anyone else. Maia knew that. Other things are harder to learn. Saw a lot of guys come home to their families and try to jump into the role of boss man in the house. Can't do that to a woman who's been running the house an' running it damn well for the last six months. Can't even do that to the kids. They look at you an' say 'Why are you telling me what to do? You're not my Mom.'

So when I came back from a stint at sea, I'd tread real careful. I'd speak to Maia, ask her what she'd like me to help out with. Took my orders from her. She never asked for much, but I'd take over the boring stuff anyways. Stuff she'd done too much of while I was gone. I'd wash dishes, mow the lawn, paint walls, bathe the kids, take her car for oil change, change diapers, cook, ask her for the shopping list, buy the stuff she needed, take the kids for walks while she got her hair done, take Greg to baseball practice, take Claire to ballet an' the like. Made sure Maia got a bit of free time to oil-paint or unwind. We'd talk about how the kids were doin' an' if I should help out with anything. Wouldn't just jump in without talking to her first. She liked the way that worked. Think she appreciated it. Made my returns from sea something she could look forward to. Beyond just the first days. Like a holiday.

Saw some of my sailor buddies whose wives couldn't wait to get them out of the house. Maia an' me we weren't like that. Worked hard to make sure that never happened.

'Nother thing. Call it fate. I actually built Greg a wooden boat when he was 'bout fourteen. He and me did it together. Took less than two weeks. Not a canoe. Something called a baidarka. Kind of kayak they used to make in the Aleutians. Greg loved it. Still has it. Still paddles it. Took it with him to San Fran.

I reckoned two weeks was quick to build it. Maia laughed at me. Said I was the slowest boat builder ever. Said it took me sixteen years to build one tiny boat. Since she and me first looked at the plans down at the chandlery.

'Nother thing, I got Maia better pay for her oil paintings. She was mad at me at first, but it worked out real well. There was this old biddy, old New England money, and lots of it. Wanted an oil painting of her daughter with her new husband. Painted from a photo of the two of them getting married, on the steps of the church. Haggled with Maia over the price of the painting. Wasn't short of money, but that was the old lady's way. Maia never haggled, just accepted that the old biddy would only pay half the usual price.

So I take the old lady one side afterwards an' says to her 'Mam, you don't want the painting of your daughter to be half price.'

She says 'Why ever not?'

I say 'Cause Maia's real skilful.'

She says 'Young man, that is the only reason I'm letting her paint my daughter.'

'Mam', I say, 'I know. But at half price, it'll be a real likeness.'

Well, the old biddy starts laughing, turns out she's not as dry as she looks. She rethinks her offer, ends up paying Maia twice the usual rate. She's real happy with the painting. Her daughter looks real pretty. Hangs it where all her friends can see. Tells them all the story. The prices on Maia's paintings go through the roof after that.

An' Maia forgave me for meddling in her painting.

You know the diary I wrote at Dildo? Did you ever get to thinkin' it was odd for a con to have a diary?

Yes – I said – a bit strange.

It was Maia – he said – that got me into the habit. Every day I was away at sea, she asked me to write something. Didn't matter ifn' it was long or short. She wanted me to write something every day, then mail her all the pages next time I touched shore. That way she said she'd get to know about my day, every day, like she'd been with me. Like we weren't apart every day. Got to be a daily habit for me.

At first I didn't know how to do it. Took me a while an' then I got her figgered out. If we were in some new port, I'd tell her what it was like to be there. What the people looked like. What they sounded like. What the food tasted like. If nothing was happening on board, I'd tell her 'bout the crew. If the cook made something good, I'd ask him about the recipe an' write it for Maia. If there was a storm I'd tell her about the storm. How the birds fly just an inch off the water. Shelter between wave crests. Had to learn a mite about birds just to write that. Used to think they were called Mother Cary's Chicks. Turns out the real name is petrel.

Was good for me too. Writing to her. Like I was speaking to her every day. Even when we were apart.

He put down the photo gently. Touched it with his fingertips, smiled at it, turned away from me and walked into the kitchen where I could no longer see him. I heard him blow his nose, clear his throat, and ask me if I wanted some more coffee. His voice was hoarse, like a man with a bad cold.

57. Claire and Maia

Later that day I told Claire what Pango had told me. We were alone outside looking at the waves, feeling the gusts tug and push at us. The gulls were riding the wind, face forward to the wind, barely having to move a wing. Just riding the gusts up and down.

"They were two lovebirds", she said. "They used to embarrass us when Greg and I were teens. Always holding hands. Mom told me she'd given up on her painting before she met Pango. She'd been going out with some artist type. It took her a while to realize what a pig he was. He wasn't the great artist he wanted to be, just mediocre and insecure. The only way he could feel great was to tell Mom what a beginner she was. She finally broke up with him a few months before she met Pango. Pango made her feel good. Pango gave her the encouragement to start again."

I hesitated, then said "what happened to her?"

Claire looked at me as though she didn't understand.

I said "I mean, how did your Mom die? If you don't mind me asking. Pango didn't say anything."

Claire sighed. "She had a leaking artery to her heart. It ballooned suddenly. Threatened to tear more. Started to leak more. They prepped her for an operation to fix it. Told all of us it was fifty/fifty at best and we should stay close."

"Were you still kids?" I asked.

"No", Claire said. "Thank goodness. We were grown up and out of the house. Greg flew back from San Fran. And thank goodness Dad was home anyway. Between ships. Long before the prison thing. He was at her bedside twenty four hours. I don't think he slept much. We were all there when she slipped away. She meant to be kind to Dad, but she did something that didn't work out so well for him in the end."

"What?" I said.

"She was holding his hand. Like always. Then she said 'Pango, I've had the best life I could ever have wished for. I've been truly lucky. Thanks to you and Greg and Claire. I couldn't have wished for anything or anyone else. If I die now, it's a small price to pay. I'm happy. So, Pango, promise me you'll not mourn me, whatever happens. Be happy for me.'

So Pango promised. What else could he do? He promised to be happy for her. But it's torn him in two pieces ever since. Pango's a man of his word. He does what he's promised. One half of him tries to be happy whenever he thinks of her. The problem is there's a buried half of him that wants to grieve and has never been able to. Poor man.

58. Revelations

The next day the weather was uncommonly calm. The Atlantic coast was a flat pond. Everett took me out with the trawler crew for two days. I got some of my best shots of the whole trip during that time. I have the photos in front of me as I write. They have a gritty industrial look to them. Black and white shots of crew members with scarred hands on the winch controls, crew members guiding huge overhead nets towards the hold, crew members knee-deep in fish shoveling ice over a new load, and some great pictures of Everett with one of the guys dismantling a problem winch at the end of the day when we were back at dock.

Gear wheels, the winch cowling, electrical switch parts and the like are strewn between them as they bend over the stripped down winch. They're totally focussed on the work and oblivious to the camera.

Once the repair was done the last of the crew went ashore. Everett stayed on a while, locking up tools and making coffee for himself and me. We ended up in the wheelhouse of the trawler. I was still peering through the Sony viewfinder looking at views of the boat and the harbour.

"Your coffee's at your elbow", Everett said. "Mind out."

I mumbled a thanks and swung the lens towards a string of four trawlers that were approaching us, on their way to their own dock.

Everett was sipping his coffee, leaning on a chart table.

"Did Pango ever tell you why he became vegetarian?"

he asked.

"Nope. Hang on a moment" I said. The light was fading and I needed to compensate. I increased the ISO setting. The Sony had surprisingly little noise even at higher ISOs.

Everett seemed to move on to a new topic while I fiddled.

"Then I guess he didn't tell you what his crime was?"

"No", I said, looking through the viewfinder at the first passing trawler. I'd need just the right moment to capture the image. Too soon, or too late, and there would be a lot of background clutter. In the middle there would be one short window of opportunity where the background promised to be wide open sky.

I think if I'd shown more interest or been looking straight at Everett, he'd have stopped or never brought it up. I've noticed before how people speak more freely when you're not looking at them directly, when you're looking into a camera that's pointed away from them. Everett fell into the same pattern. Seemed to need to tell me just because I wasn't looking at him.

"He wouldn't tell you", he said. "He won't mind me telling you, but he'll never speak of it himself".

I finally put down the camera and looked at him.

"What happened" I asked.

"You know that Pango was a sailor. Ocean going ships all around the globe?"

"Yes."

"After a long stretch away, he ended up signing onto an FOC ship. That's a flag of convenience ship, registered to some third world country or similar.

What happens is a ship owner has to register his ship with a country. The ship owner pays taxes to that country and follows the laws and standards of that country. That includes the labour laws for how to pay and treat a ship's crew, and what safety standards to follow at sea.

Good ship owners mostly register with the country they reside in. Bad ship owners usually look for an FOC. They look for a country to register where the taxes are cheap, the standards are low, the inspection and enforcement of standards are a farce, where the labour laws allow the owner to pay the crew next to nothing, and where, if the crew ever brought a case to court, the owner has near certainty of winning.

Who knows why Pango did it. Sailors with any sense, and Pango has plenty, avoid an FOC ship.

Maybe he was in a hurry to get somewhere. Maybe the next stop for the FOC ship was somewhere he needed to get to quickly. Maybe its next stop was in a port where he had a decent ship waiting for him if he could get there in time. He'd also gotten a reckless streak after his wife died. Like he didn't care anymore. There are many possibilities. I don't know. Pango told me what he was comfortable telling me, and I've never dug for more details.

However it happened then, he was on an FOC ship of the worst kind.

The ship got into a heavy blow off the Southern African coast and the engine quit. No electrical power either after the engine quit. The radio room should have had a spare power system, but it turned out the ship had been stripped of any saleable auxiliary equipment. Probably sold off either by the owner or a previous captain or one of the previous officers. Sea anchors had been sold, auxiliary batteries and generators had been sold, and, as it later turned out most of the survival gear in the lifeboats had been sold off. Gone. Without power the radio was dead. The storm worsened and the bow got smashed by a heavy wave. Crumpled and stove in like paper.

Ships are designed for a certain lifespan and a certain environment. Say 30 years for Mediterranean sailing. The marine architect will then specify a hull thickness to withstand most Mediterranean conditions you'd expect to find in 30 years of sailing. And as a margin of error the design would include some even bigger Med waves that you might encounter even in, say, fifty years of sailing.

Trouble begins if the ship is already fifty years old, has used up its nine lives, is still sailing, and runs into a one-in-sixty-years wave that it wasn't designed for. Or it's put into service in the open Atlantic. Even worse, if some past or present owner has decided to make uncertified modifications. Perhaps takes out a safety bulkhead here or there to increase cargo room. Perhaps adds a heavy crane up on the deck which moves the centre of mass up and forward. Perhaps adds an extra through-hull fitting here or there.

Mind you, the hull on this death trap was probably razor thin too after years of rust had gone unchecked and uninspected. FOC ships often don't get much inspection or maintenance.

The captain and crew took to lifeboats. Pango ended up in a smaller lifeboat with five others. They were blown far south off the commercial shipping routes. When they opened the storage lockers on the lifeboat, they found that the standard emergency rations, flares, bailers, portable radio, desalination gear, fishing tackle, water, emergency rations etc. was all missing. Stripped and sold off. They had a hard time of it."

Everett looked at me and seemed to change tack.

"Do you know much of modern day piracy?" he asked.

"Not much" – I said. "I hear it exists off the coast of Somalia."

"More than that", said Everett. "I'm an inshore trawler man, strictly local, but I read. I keep up to date. Recent figures are about 200 attacks a year near Malacca and the Singapore Straits, 20 attacks per year off the coast of Somalia, and 70 attacks of the west coast of Africa, near Guinea, and in total about 200 hostages still held. Off Malacca and Singapore they don't take hostages, just push sailors into the sea."

"Those don't sound like the regions where Pango's lifeboat was drifting."

"No", said Everett. "What I'm saying is that things that you read about as a kid, Robinson Crusoe, pirates, Blackbeard, Edward Teach, press gangs, ship wrecks, marooning and the like still happen in this day and age.

They happen, because, when you strip out the modern radio and desalination gear from a life boat, the sailors that are left in the boat are no different from sailors two or three centuries ago. So these things still happen. Not as often, but they happen. They happened on Pango's life boat.

The story of his lifeboat gets bad now."

He hesitated and fiddled with his coffee mug. "Should I continue?"

"Yes", I said. "I'd like to know."

"After six days drifting things looked bleak. Aside from exposure to the elements, they were starving and dying of thirst. They'd been able to catch a little rain water, but not enough. Three of the men – not Pango - started to discuss a lottery. It's an idea as old as the first shipwreck.

They said 'is it better that six men die, or that one is eaten and five survive?'

They meant that the lottery victim would not only provide food, but also water – in the form of blood and water content in the flesh. The human body is two thirds water. Water is what the men in the lifeboat needed most.

One of the men, another American as it happens, had started to drink sea water, which was going to kill him more quickly than if he'd held off. Two days after the first discussion of the lottery, he was in a coma."

Everett paused. We looked out of the wheelhouse windows. Lights were coming on around us and Everett's trawler was rocking in the wake of the second passing trawler. We bumped a little against the dock wall fenders with each wave. The passing trawler had its running lights on now for the fading daylight. Two white masthead lights, and the red port light visible to us. We could hear the diesel motor and its exhaust burbling along next to us. The voices from the crew carried over the water to us, reflected up to us by the water.

Everett said "trawlers have to show a green masthead light over the white masthead light when they're trawling. No port and starboard running lights if they're trawling and stationary."

He seemed to be hunting for a neutral topic.

"So what happened", I asked.

He took a last glance at the passing trawler.

"The next morning one of the men who'd been discussing a lottery, strangled the comatose fellow. Among the others, two including Pango, protested, but did not physically intervene. This was confirmed by others later at the trial.

The men who'd been discussing a lottery said again 'is it better that five men die, or that we use the food we have?'

All five, Pango included, ate.

Everett sighed. "It's getting late", he said. "Claire will be expecting us for dinner. I think I'm putting you off dinner, maybe putting you off Pango or staying with us any longer. I don't know why I started on this. Except..."

"What?" I said.

"I didn't want you staying with us in ignorance. It would be worse to keep it from a houseguest and have it surprise him later. Pango's business is his, but if you're my houseguest I'm responsible for you too."

"Thank you," I said. "Anyway. I wanted to know. I feel sorry for Pango. He's a decent man who was caught up in something he couldn't hope to control. He never hid the key facts from me, that he was a convict for manslaughter. Never hid the fact that he felt guilty. I imagine after eight days of raging thirst, most people are capable of anything to survive. What happened next?"

"Let me phone Claire to say we'll be late".

The third in the line of approaching trawlers was abeam of us. In addition to all the other waterborne sounds we could hear the garbled marine radio from their wheelhouse, and a voice saying "Isabella switching to channel 88".

The passing trawler had switched on its deck lights. I could see crew men standing ready at the bow and stern with huge mooring lines ready to dock the trawler. They looked up at our wheelhouse as they passed. We hadn't lit our wheelhouse yet, but they could see our silhouettes inside.

Everett stepped out of the wheelhouse to make his cell phone call to Claire. I didn't hear their conversation. He stepped back inside closing his cell phone and turned back to me.

"The five survived long enough to be picked up by a Netherlands flagged chemicals tanker that had also been forced south by the blow. The tanker scooped the men out of the boat and brought them to safety. Two of the five men were delirious and in the sick bay they both raved about eating a comrade. The issue went to the captain who questioned the three others. Of course the story came out.

The chemicals tanker was bound for Houston. The captain notified the FBI who were waiting to arrest the five."

I was puzzled. "Did US jurisdiction apply?" I asked.

Everett sipped his now cold coffee. "There was a lot of discussion before and during the trial about jurisdiction. The FBI and the prosecution were clear, and satisfied the court. The US can extend jurisdiction for crimes at high sea under several circumstances, even when the crime is committed on a vessel under a foreign flag.

Two of those circumstances applied in Pango's case. The first is that the offender or the victim or both are US citizens. That alone would have clinched it.

The second circumstance that applied is that the victim or perpetrator are on a vessel that departed from or will arrive at a US port. That was less clear because the original vessel did not qualify. But the rescue vessel did.

In the end the court ruled that since Pango was a US national, by these rules, he fell under US jurisdiction. The non-US nationals were deported to their countries of origin.

The judge put a publication ban in place for the sake of the victim's family. It would have been too easy to sensationalize the crime."

"I feel sorry for Pango", I said again. "It's like you said, something out of Robinson Crusoe. He got caught in something ugly out of another century. Something that should never have happened in this day and age."

"When I called Claire just now", Everett said, "I let her know that I was telling you the full story. Said you'd need some time to mull it over. So rather than go straight home to join them, we'll go have a light dinner down on the dock, or just a coffee, or a beer. Whatever you feel like. They'll have their meal back home without us. We'd still like you to stay with us, but if you feel you can't after what you've heard, let me know and we'll understand."

Everett and I had a pizza down at the dock, and a coffee. Then we drove back to Jonathon, Clair and Pango. We never spoke of Pango's crime again. I stayed another four days. My main memory of Pango from those four days is not Everett's story, but of the next evening, with Pango sitting at supper beaming.

Claire is on his right, holding onto his right hand, just as she used to when she was little. She's quite unaware that Pango can't eat at all, that he can't use his left hand. Jonathon is sitting in a high chair to Pango's left, holding Pango's left hand. That's another photo I have spread in front of me as I write.

59. The Parcel

After I got home I was in touch a few times with Pango, mainly by phone, to chat.

Claire also sent me a card thanking me for bringing Pango home. The card also contained a photo of two tiny orange kittens with a short explanation from Claire. She wrote:

"Pango found these two kittens in a local animal rescue shelter. He had a long talk with me and Everett about whether we'd be willing to take them into our house. It wasn't normally something we'd have done, or at least not while Jonathan was still quite young, but Dad doesn't often ask for anything, and for whatever reason this seemed very important to him. So Everett and I said 'fine'. It seemed to take a weight off Dad's mind. I don't recall any previous special feeling Dad ever had for cats. He told us though, he's been visiting animal shelters for a while here in Portland looking for the right cats, whatever that means. Dad didn't say much about why or what made them right. Everettt thinks maybe Dad saw the animal rescue shelter as a prison for the animals and wanted the cats out of there. Whatever his reasons, we've become very glad that we agreed. The kittens are adorable and have won us over, Jonathan included. The kittens spend all evening wrestling each other. It's all in good fun and high spirits and a great show to watch. Dad spoils them rotten. Almost as much as he spoils Jonathan. Dad has named the kittens Anand and Stavros. "

I didn't tell Claire what I knew about the kittens. That would be up to Pango, whenever he was ready to talk about his darker days in Dildo Correctional. I guessed he was still in celebration mode with his daughter and keeping the stories lighthearted. I did send Everett a large print of the photo showing him and his crew-man bent over the dismantled winch. I gathered the photo was a big hit. Everett hung it in his study.

They invited me to come down the following May and do some more photography on Everett's trawler.

Then Pango set off to visit Gregory, his son, in San Francisco for a few months. I said let's touch base when you get back to Maine.

About the time that Pango was due back in Maine I was out of touch, in Europe, for over a month. When I got back there was a letter and a parcel from Claire waiting for me.

The letter said:

I tried your office phone. The message said you'd be gone until December. The switchboard lady wouldn't give me your cell phone number but you'll want to know about this when you get back, so I'm writing.

You remember the last evening before you left us? Pango was telling us his theory that his health is fine; that his friend Cory scammed the medical reports and x-ray images that were sent to the prison doctor; that Cory was using the same trick that he used to get himself free, to get Pango free; that Cory had found a way to hack the medical files for Pango and edit the test results.

You didn't say much either way. I think you felt, like Everett and me, that Pango was doing some wishful thinking. None of us said it to Pango, we didn't want to raise the possibility that he really was dying. We all hoped he was right.

While Pango was in SF visiting Gregory and his wife Angie - and they had a great time together - Pango's health went down, fast. The prison doctor's health report was right, after all. There was no Cory scam.

Pango got back to Maine in November. The travel took a lot more out of him. He wasn't good. We took Pango to our GP. He reviewed the prison medical reports and gave Pango meds for the pain.

Pango didn't want to go into hospital or a hospice. Said they were kinder institution than prison but the similarities were too scary for him. Said the paperwork, the institutional routines and the hierarchies would again become more important than the man.

He also had a bad experience when our GP suggested he ought to consult a dietician who is attached to the hospital. She - the dietician - tried to argue with him that, with all his body was fighting, he couldn't afford to be short on major food groups or have a limited diet.

You know how Pango is physically and psychologically incapable of ever eating meat, ever again. He nearly died of starvation in Bilbo when they tried to force the issue with him. I'm rambling, but you get where I'm going. The dietician was just another black mark against hospitals in his eyes.

We made him comfortable here at home, and he died where he wanted to be, without much distress at the end of November. And as usual with Pango, his main concern was he didn't want to be a burden on us. In truth, he wasn't.

Everett and I are hesitating about whether I should let someone at Bilbo know about Dad's death. Everett thinks Bilbo is a closed chapter in Pango's life that should be left closed. I think it might be good to let Mrs. Haverman know.

She worked with him for years, was a friend to him, and would let some of his other friends there, as well as her daughter, know. What do you think?

Finally, the parcel is something he said he wanted you to have.

Call us when you're back.
Love
Claire, Everett, Jonathan, Stavros and Anand.

Claire had attached a short obituary from the local Portland paper. It said simply:

Philip Andrew Norman George (known as 'Pango') Brown, passed away peacefully on Sunday night surrounded by family. Philip is survived and deeply missed by his son Gregory Brown, his daughter in-law, Angie Brown, his daughter Claire Veilleux, his son in-law Everett Veilleux and his grandson Jonathon Veilleux.

The parcel was neatly wrapped in brown grease paper. There was no note attached. From the neatness of the wrapping I suspect that it was Claire who had wrapped it.

Inside I found The Child's Book of Victorian Parlour Games, 1878-1888, Volume 3, By Edgar G. Greenlock, reprinted 1907 by Jonathan Harper and Sons.

60. Acknowledgements

First, thanks to my friend of many years, Daphne Cooper, who read an early draft of this book and offered suggestions and encouragement. Daphne is herself a superb writer – along with many other accomplishments - and her input was invaluable.

Second, thanks to my wife and family for letting me have the time and space to write this.

Last and not least, I mention two organizations in this book that are concerned with improving the quality of justice and legal systems. The two organizations mentioned, EJI and The National Registry of Exonerations, are real and not fictional. My thanks to the men and women of these and similar organizations the world over. Their efforts makes the world a better place.

61. Other Books By Peter Staadecker

Watch for "Just One More Page" coming in 2017.

For more information about this book, and about the author, please visit the author's website:

http://publishing.staadecker.com

62. Contact The Author

Fan? Or want to be on the distribution list for news about Peter's books and book contests? Drop Peter a note. You can reach him via his website at:

http://publishing.staadecker.com/index.php#contact

(Please do not send suggestions for a plot – Peter will delete those unread.)